I0720434

KOJI A. DAE

MAZI

MAZI

Copyright © 2024 Koji A. Dae

First published in Great Britain 2024
by Ghost Orchid Press

ISBN (paperback): 978-1-7390918-1-1
ISBN (e-book): 978-1-7390918-0-4

Cover illustration © Claire L. Smith
Book formatting by Claire Saag

CHAPTER ONE

The yantra house is nothing like the photos. Most Airbnbs embellish, but where the pictures had shown a cute cottage in a sunlit clearing, the actual villa can best be described as a shack. The sweet white table surrounded by manicured flowers that I imagined having morning coffee at is overgrown with running vines of ivy and thick tangles of nettles that bite at my jeans. I hiss and dance around them, wishing I had worn boots as I pick my way towards the wooden porch that wraps around the small house.

Philip leans on the Kia's driver-side door and gives a low whistle. "They definitely don't check the honesty of these adverts."

"No such thing as false advertising in Bulgaria," I tell him.

The forest leans in towards the house, every hint of a path covered with underbrush. The small asphalt driveway narrows to a bottleneck so tight it looks as if it's closing in on itself, sealing us in this little patch of land. Maybe it wouldn't be so bad if the sun was out, but an autumn storm has been threatening to brew all day, coating the sky in a thick blanket of dark gray clouds, always a few minutes away from rain.

"I don't think we'll do much hiking," I say with a pout.

"Well, I didn't think we would anyway." Philip gives me

one of his overly dramatic winks as he slams his door. His decisive stride and the sight of his broad shoulders filling out his t-shirt put me at ease. This week will be fine. It isn't about the villa. It's about us. It's been so hard settling into our apartment these past few months. A weekend away will do us good.

I take another step, and there's the unmistakable rustling of a small animal in the nearby grass. I freeze mid-stride and squint to find what I assume is a lizard. Mid-October; I thought it was too late for them to still be scurrying about. After thirty seconds, there's still no movement. I carefully put my foot down, but as soon as the grass bends, the rustle comes again.

This time I find the creature and let out a long, high-pitched scream.

Philip is around the car and at my side almost instantly, but still not fast enough to see the thick body of the snake as it slithers away.

"What is it?" he asks.

"A snake," I whisper, still frozen in place.

"This late in the season? It can't be."

"I swear, right there." I point to a dense clump of grass. "I mean, it's gone now, but it was there."

He rubs my lower back. "Well, the grass is pretty over-grown. I guess we'll have to be careful."

I nod, but still can't seem to move.

He rubs my back harder. "Come on, let's check out the house."

I allow him to take my hand and follow him up the stone steps to the porch, which squeaks in protest at our combined weight. Philip gives a little hop and the whole structure vibrates. I cling to the railing. Rough swellings of the old wood jut into my tense palms, threatening to splinter into my skin as I wait for him to jostle the structure again.

But he must notice my pale face, because instead he comes close and wraps his arms around me. I breathe his cologne, which somehow smells distinctly American even though Old Spice has been available in Bulgaria for years.

"No getting frisky out here," he mumbles against my hair, nuzzling down towards my neck. "One of your orgasms would bring the whole thing down."

Leaning on the railing, my back against him, I indulge in the fantasy of looking over the quiet forest while rutting like animals. A small flash of light flickers in the distance, and I feel more than hear the answering rumble. I let my head fall onto his shoulder and sigh. "I suppose not."

"Let's look inside," he says as the first fat raindrops fall on the porch.

The front door is unlocked. Inside there's a hook latch, but no key on the entryway table as the owner promised. Not that we have to lock the villa. We're twenty kilometers from the nearest village, and even that was just a hamlet of mostly unoccupied houses and a single general store. We had stopped to buy ice (of which there was none) and the final cold beers from the fridge. The lady behind the counter had eyed us suspiciously, but hadn't asked where we were from or where we were going. It's unlikely anyone except the owner of the villa even knows we're here.

My chest tightens at the thought. I sent the listing to Krisi when we booked it, but the link had no address. Directions came last night—cutting it so close I almost cancelled—and I hadn't bothered to forward them before we left. I pull my phone from my hoodie pocket and press the button to light up the screen. On the top right corner are the dreaded two dashes. I groan.

"No service?" Philip asks.

"Of course not," I snap, putting the phone back in my pocket.

"Hey now, no taking it out on me." His tone is playful, but when he lifts my sullen chin his eyes are hard. Demanding.

"Yes, sir." My stomach tingles at the words, and he gives the slightest nod of approval, the dark scruff at the corners of his mouth twitching in a smile.

The floor is worn wood with a faded runner covering the middle, and I don't want to take my shoes off. Years of living in the States tell me it's okay to keep them on. The floor is probably filthy anyway. But Philip wedges his off, and I follow his lead. Even through my damp socks, I can feel the deep grime flattening the fibers of the hand-woven carpet.

Exploring the first floor takes two steps and a head-turn in each direction. Two small rooms on either side of the entry hall. The kitchen consists of a stained sink, an old refrigerator with a questionable scent when I open it, and an even older cast-iron stove.

"Tell me that's not wood-burning."

Philip opens one of the iron doors, which creaks in protest. Ash fills the bottom of the small chamber. "You mean you didn't cook on these every summer growing up?"

I swat him playfully. "You know I was never a village girl."

It's a lie. While I spent the school year in the city, my parents shipped me off to my grandparents' village in the summer, where I spent the long, hot days avoiding stray dogs and the older boys who had long since tired of tormenting farm animals.

"Well, then we'll figure it out together." Which means he'll figure it out and teach me. It's how we navigate the world—from a new shopping center to a party I'm unsure of. He goes first and paves the way for me.

He leads me into the other room, which is set up as a living, dining, and bedroom combination. I've seen this same room a dozen times with only small variations. Perhaps the tapestry that turns the single bed into a couch during the day was green instead of blue and gold. Or maybe the plastic table cloth had purple flowers instead of faded roses with brown stems. But the rooms are so similar, it's as if I'm standing in all of them at once. They all smell of old people—impending death, plastic shelf-liner, and stuffed cabbage rolls.

"Charming," Philip says.

I sigh and wrap my arms across my chest. Philip and I moved into a new apartment last year. I insisted on a new build. Something modern that smelled of fresh paint. All new furniture, mostly from Ikea. Nothing traditionally Bulgarian despite Philip's adoration of our classic pottery and his fascination with my mother's needlepoint. It wasn't shame. Not quite. I was just exhausted of the post-communist style that never seemed to change, all rooms variations on the same theme. I wanted something unique. Something that was just ours. He didn't have to point out the irony of me finding that individuality in flat-pack furniture that propagated around the world. But he did.

"Oh come on." He takes my hand and gives it a squeeze. "What's one thing you like here?"

I look carefully around the room. Thin strips of wood panel the lower half of the walls. The upper half is painted in sloppy whitewash. A landscape needlepoint stretches across the back of the bed. The details of green hills and yellow rapeseed fields must have taken a lifetime. A large, open fireplace dominates the opposite corner, with a single row of bricks looping around its gaping maw to partition its ash-covered stones from the bare wooden floor. A bench is built into the wall next to it, and it runs the length of the room, ending in a quaint cabinet filled with books and small trinkets. Wood for the fire fills the space below the bench, and I can't help but imagine spiders and beetles nesting in the cracks.

"Do you want to just leave?" He releases me and runs his hands through his short curls. "We can probably make it home before dark if we go now."

I consider the winding mountain pass we crossed to get here, and the last twenty kilometers of switchbacks. I made Philip stop twice so I could slow the dizzying of my head and quiet the churning in my stomach. I definitely don't want to cross that narrow wooden bridge that, I swear, swayed even beneath our tiny car.

"The beams are nice," I admit. Two wooden beams, at least twenty-five centimeters wide, span the ceiling of the room. Another one splits the hall, and two more are in the kitchen. They are dark, stained almost black, and seem solid compared to the creaking of the house. "They'd be good for suspension."

Philip stares at me, wrinkles his eyebrows, then gives a bark of laughter. "Too bad we didn't bring any hooks."

"Or rope," I say.

"Bet we could find some in the maza."

I roll my eyes. Philip speaks Bulgarian well enough to get by when we go out, but we rarely use it between us. English is just easier. He has some Bulgarian words he just loves, though, maza being one of them. He likes that it sounds like maze, as if anytime he opens a cellar door he might find a magical labyrinth waiting for him. For a man who doesn't believe in magic, he certainly has a bit of romance to him. Not that he would ever admit it.

We don't go in search of the maza, though. There's no stairs going down, which means the entrance must be on the outside, and rain is pelting the windows now. Instead, we find the narrow, winding staircase at the far side of the hall that takes us to the second floor.

The single room seems more well-cared for than the first floor. One corner has a small, cylindrical stove with a pile of chopped wood in a basket next to it. We'll have to start a fire soon. The storm had held in a bit of summer heat, but now that it has broken, the air is chilled. Within a few hours, I'll be cold. Then cranky.

I cross to the stove, but Philip makes straight for the double bed pushed beneath the peak of the room, which boasts an even larger wooden beam than the ones downstairs, this one blond with light knots throughout. Two wooden posts support the main crossbeam, and a large, white rug rests between them. It's thick, and I nuzzle my wet toes into the long fibers, warming them.

"Not bad," he says, pressing on the mattress, which springs beneath his weight.

The corner above the kitchen is a surprisingly large bathroom with a double sink and large jacuzzi tub. It's walled off with glass panels.

"Because pooping in front of your partner is so romantic," I say, pointing to the exposed toilet and crossing the room to get a better look.

"Oh, hush." Philip loops an arm out and tackles me to

the bed. The mattress gives a little, but there's no squeaking. The bed is solid, at least.

I wriggle out of his grasp and scoot to the head of the bed, waiting for him to recapture me. He obliges, pinning my wrists above my head with one of his hands, the length of his muscular body pressed against me so I can feel our heat mingling through our sweatshirts and jeans. I reach my face up, trying to cover his mouth with mine, but he pulls away.

"Silvena," he says, drawing back so I can see the seriousness of his face. "We'll be fine here. It'll be a fun two weeks."

I sigh and twist out of his grasp. He lets me go, and we both sit with our backs against the wooden headboard.

"I know."

"You were the one who thought a digital detox would do us good," he reminds me. "No phones. No work. No distraction."

"Just you and me," I agree. There's also a bag of board games in the car, but those don't count as a distraction. They're more like facilitators. Something we can tell our friends we did when they ask how the getaway went.

"Then why are you so disappointed?"

I run my thumbs together, feeling the waxiness of my skin. "It just feels so old. I don't know what I expected—a villa in the middle of nowhere, in Bulgaria. But the pictures made it seem fresh. Something new. Now it just feels like we're living the same experience a hundred other couples have lived."

"And so what if we are?" Philip asks. "We're living it as ourselves, and that's something no one else has done before."

"I guess you're right." I want to make him understand how the decades-old furniture makes me feel. Life settles differently in these long-kept rooms. It echoes on the ledges like a faint layer of dust, and I fear I'll breathe in memories that aren't my own. But he would say it's more of my Saturday-child nonsense—the grandiose fantasies of communicating with the unseen that Baba planted in my head since before I could walk. He'd be right. I don't really believe in ghosts. Spirits, maybe. God, yes. But not ghosts.

"Of course I'm right." He grins and I reach up to stroke his stubble.

"It's just that we're so far out here. All alone." I bite my lip, trying to find the right words to make him understand. "The forest feels like it's closing in on this place, and the house … it just feels suffocating."

He strokes my thick hair and tries to tuck it behind my ear, but as usual it insists on being the one part of my body that won't obey him.

"The weather isn't helping with that. But tomorrow we'll open some windows, get some fresh air. You'll feel better."

He's right. I know he is. But there's still a feeling niggling at the edge of my brain. "It's the isolation. No one around for miles and yet, or maybe because of that, I feel like someone's watching us."

"No one is watching us," he says. "I keep telling you not to watch those horror movies. They get in your head."

"It's not the movies," I say, even though I did sneak one last week when he was out late with friends. "It's like being the only humans for so far around puts us on display."

"Mm," he murmurs. A single finger strokes up my thigh. It skips to my chest, runs up the bones of my breastplate, and finds the bare skin of my neck. "And how does that make you feel, being on display?"

I stare past his square jawline at the two wood columns in the center of the room. His fingers are warm on my neck, and they make me ache for more of his touch. Anyone else would think he had gotten bored with my rambling and was trying to distract me, but I know this is how he listens, so I consider my answer carefully. "I feel scared. My heart goes faster."

"Scared?" He pushes my hair back again and adjusts so he can nibble my neck. His words bounce off my bare skin. "Your heart also goes faster when you're excited, doesn't it?"

I nod.

He stops nuzzling against me long enough to remove my hoodie and the clammy t-shirt beneath it. My nipples perk at the cold air, and he takes advantage of my newly exposed skin, stroking my breastplate with his fingertips and lips. "Are you excited now?"

I swallow and nod.

"Tell me, Silvena." I can hear his smile. "What does it feel like to be excited?"

The familiarity of the game he's playing eases the last of my anxiety. I take a breath and hold it in my chest, feeling the way my body expands in the expectation of the moment.

"My skin feels cold. Almost wet."

I trace his jeans, the ribbed texture echoing my finger-prints.

"My fingertips tingle."

There's a heat in my chest, and it rises to my throat, swelling my tongue and making my voice thick. "I want to kiss you."

He cups his hand at the nape of my neck, entwining his

fingers in my thick hair. He pulls back steadily, opening my neck to him. I give a low moan.

He nips at my skin, sending a thrilling pin of pain down my chest. "I didn't ask what you want. Tell me how you feel. Scared?"

My fear has been pushed out by anticipation and desire. Where just five minutes ago I felt as if I was Alice, shrinking fast in a wonderland I couldn't control, now my body expands. It oozes, soaking up touch and taste and the vague scent of mothballs and old fires.

"No," I say. "Not anymore."

He licks from my collarbone to my earlobe and whispers. "Then tell me."

"My stomach is light. Almost metallic."

Spit fills my mouth, and I swallow it.

"Like aluminum foil between my teeth. Those excited, sharp twinges. The ones that ache too sweetly."

Describing it drives the sensation through my body. It shoots lower. "And they go down to my pussy."

His open palm circles my belly, then he unbuttons my jeans and plunges his hand into them.

"Everything feels wet. And hot."

"Hot?" His fingers separate my folds and find the slickness I'm talking about. "You just said you feel cold."

My hips grind upwards, helping him find the edge of my clit, then further up, teasing at the idea of inviting him into me.

"Cold and hot at once. Like ice that's on fire."

My eyes dart across the room to the stove. We should have started the fire before getting in bed. Warmed up the room so we can be naked all week. Just skin and blankets and the smell of dry wood.

Philip makes a few harder strokes, his fingertips curling to cup my perineum while his flat palm pushes into me, pulling me back to my body.

"Now," he relents, "you can tell me what you want."

He removes his hand from my pussy and a fierce need for it makes my stomach clench. But he's at my jeans, peeling them off and throwing them on the floor. My underwear follow. I'm naked and he's fully clothed, kneeling above me on the bed.

I take my time. It'd be easy to ask a dozen things from him. His tongue inside me, his mouth kissing my skin. His lips on mine. His fingernails scraping welts into my flesh. His cock rubbing against my clit. Slipping inside. He would give me any of these.

He doesn't make a move to undress. He doesn't anticipate or sway my desires with his own. He waits, staring at me. His lips curl with pleasure at my indecision, and suddenly I know what I want.

"I want people to look at me the way you do. I want an audience."

His smile melts into a grin, and his eyes flash with excitement. It's taken years, but I've learned not to ask for the easy things.

He sits back on his heels and looks around the room. Then suddenly he's down against me again, the length of his muscular body pressed tight to mine, only his clothes separating me from him. I press harder, trying to bypass the fabric and get at his heat. He points to the beam above us.

"You see that knot there?"

I follow where he's pointing. A large knot, the size of a tomato, stands out pale blond against the wood. "That's a woman. Watching us."

I squint and the blob takes the vague outline of a face with two darker eyes. The center of the knot, a little rosebud of brightness, becomes an open mouth, shocked at my nudity.

"There's another." Philip points to a smaller knot on the nearest pillar. "Watching what I'm doing to you."

With that, his hand busies itself at my pussy again. As he curls his fingers to slide into me, working them slowly against my g-spot, I find all the knots in the room. There's three above us, looking down on our act like angels observing the filth of humanity. The two on the pillar are less judgmental. One looks on with longing, the other with awe. She can't believe what we're doing, but if she was twenty years younger, she'd also be opening her legs to this strange audience.

"Are they watching you?" Philip's voice is thick. My hips work in motion with his fingers, grinding over him, and I moan low and guttural.

"Yes," I say.

"You like them watching you."

I inhale sharply. He stops. Holds until I breathe again, then continues more slowly. Building once again.

"Yes."

"Tell me about them."

"They're all women," I say. "Three above." I gasp. "Two across." A small moan competes with my description, but I push through it. "One wants to look away but can't." I stare at the second, smaller one. Her wooden mouth seems to grow wider as I watch. "Another wishes she was me. They all wish—" another gasp "—they all want to be doing this. With you."

"With us?" he prompts.

"Yes. They want to feel this pleasure. They want to be ripped open for the world to see. They want to be …"

I'm so close, but he slows, drawing a whimper from me.

"Say it," he demands.

"They want to be …" He goes faster and I lose the word again.

He slows and the edging is almost painful. I cry out.

"Say it!"

"They want …" His hand starts moving again, and I lose the words. "To be …"

He presses hard into me, waiting.

"Exposed," I gasp.

He gives a final jerk and I start to come. Hot liquid gushes between my legs and I press onto his fingers, moaning. His movements are minimal, letting me work out the final spasms of my orgasm on my own.

When I stop moving, he carefully removes his hand and lays it on my damp pubic hair. The scent of me blends with the old must of the room, breathing life into the house.

I open my eyes, unsure of when I closed them. He leans back and pulls me onto his chest. His sweater is warm and soft, but I wish I could feel his skin against mine. I'll have to get him out of it. But for now I lie in the gentle buzz of pleasure he created in me.

"Better?" he asks.

"Mmmhmmm," I murmur.

He strokes my hair lightly. "I told you, this week will be just fine."

"Yeah," I agree. "As long as we don't get out of bed."

He kisses the top of my head. "So we won't."

CHAPTER TWO

I wake to the heavy silence of nature—the sound of trees creaking in the breeze and the memory of a bird hooting in the distance. The silver moon casts long shadows around the room. Philip's arm is heavy on my stomach, and he snores slightly. I roll over to lie on my back, staring up at the dark ceiling.

I hold my breath in my mouth, rolling it over my tongue, then puff it out in a little cloud. The warm mist is just visible in the chilled air. Last night we barely got out of bed to unload the bags from the car. The groceries went to the kitchen and the clothes in open suitcases in one corner. We couldn't be bothered with the low chest of drawers. Then it was back under the covers, me returning the favor of release. We fell asleep before starting a fire, and now the joints in my fingers ache from the cold. I pull my hands under the blanket and snuggle closer to Philip.

My cheek lands in a damp patch of drool and I scoot away in disgust. The bodily fluids I usually beg for are less attractive when cold and congealed. I throw my feet over the side of the bed. My toes curl against the icy floor, but I force myself to stand and approach the small stove.

The wood in the basket is sorted by size, large pieces as thick as my forearm on one side and sticks of kindling on the other. I find a metal hook and open the top of the stove.

It reveals a black hole that seems to stretch impossibly long. I put my hand into the opening, my white skin engulfed by darkness. I hold it there for a second. The belly of the stove has a thick emptiness that makes my skin vibrate. When I can't stand it any longer, I snatch my hand back.

I haven't lit a fire since I was a kid, and even then it was mostly handing pieces of wood to my dyado as he arranged them. I can't remember whether I'm supposed to start with the large pieces or small ones.

Philip turns on the bed, and I think about waking him. He's got the camping experience—thru-hiking trails I can only imagine. He'd know how to approach this. But it'd be nice to surprise him with a warm room. Maybe even breakfast.

I lower a mix of wood into the stove, layering logs and kindling next to each other, hoping they'll strike a magic balance and ignite. The stack of newspapers next to the basket seems to be from twenty years ago, when newspapers had as many naked women as girlie magazines. I ball one woman's legs closed and shove her into the kindling. The long match catches on her nipples, and the dry paper sparks to life.

Breathing on the flames makes old ash swirl up. I should have figured out how to empty the stove before starting. Too late now. I purse my lips together and coax the flame to life with another breath.

Finally, a crackle of wood. Then a pop. The fire catches. Just watching the orange flames lick the dry wood makes me warmer. I plunk the metal cover in place with a sense of satisfaction.

When I turn back to the room, I almost expect it to be lit and cheery. But the fire is contained to the cylinder with no glass to share its light, and it's just as dark and still as it was moments ago. I move to the pillar nearest the bed to grab my discarded hoodie. Touching the time-worn wood, I remember yesterday's ecstasy and try to find one of my women.

The knot is hard and smooth beneath my fingers. I lean close, tracing the woodgrain with my gaze. There, her eyes. And there, her mouth, open and round. But in the dark morning, it no longer looks like she's moaning with pleasure. The mouth is too wide. Gaping.

I let my hand fall away, but the face remains etched as clearly as a painting.

She's screaming.

A creature echoes her sound. An owl? A mountain lion? I don't know, but all I hear is the screech of terror.

My heart pounds and I back away from the pillar. The sound fades. I take a deep breath.

"It's just your imagination," I tell myself, then get dressed and head down to see about breakfast.

By the time I descend the narrow staircase, watery light is filtering through the windows, the day pushing away my nighttime fears. But the idea of wrestling with another fire is too much. I'll leave breakfast to Philip. At least the house is modern enough to have an espresso machine so I don't have to boil coffee in the mocha pot hanging behind the stove. I turn the machine on and pull a strong cup into a tiny ceramic mug. It's one of those traditional ones, meant for sipping shipka tea. Its body is the classic red of clay, and the swirled paint around the rim is blue and green with a thick splash of white that reminds me of the cum I swallowed last night. I let my thumb trace the paint. I can see why Philip likes the traditional ceramics. They have a certain character to them. More than our plain white mugs at home. Maybe I'll give in and let him buy a set for our apartment.

A splash of milk and a pinch of stevia, and the morning isn't so bad.

I take my cup to the rackety porch and watch the sun rise from behind the forest. It lights the clearing in oranges and pinks. Everything is still and quiet, and the light burns off the thin layer of fog, warming my shoulders. The heat turns the dew into an oppressive layer of humidity, and it almost feels as if I'm still stuffed in the tiny house.

I turn to look at it. Its roof is lopsided, the plaster falling off to reveal thin bones of wood. It might not be much, but this week it's ours—a universe of solitude.

A sharp thud cuts through my reverie. I tense. Another thud, and a crack.

My fingers grip my mug. It's coming from the side of the house.

Thud. Thud. It's more rhythmic.

I want to yell for Philip. Or creep back up the stairs to the safety of his arms.

But that's silly. I'm a grown woman. I can handle …

Thud. Crack. Thud. Thud.

What is that?

I leave my coffee on the railing and descend the stairs to the bumpy grass, keeping close to the house to avoid the nettles.

Around the corner, a short, wooden door hangs open. The gaps between the wood are so large I can almost make out the figure behind it. A large ax swings down, dark metal glinting in the morning sun. It hits a piece of wood stood lengthwise on a low, fat log. The wood comes up with the ax and then it all swings down again. Thunk-crack all at once.

I clear my throat, but the swinging barely pauses long enough for a hand to place another piece of wood on the log.

I skirt the door, giving a wide berth to the swinging ax and tiny pieces of wood that split off in all directions with every blow.

The man powering the ax is tall. His shoulders aren't as broad as Philip's but obvious ropes of muscle strain against his cream button-up shirt. The sleeves are rolled to his elbows, the top two buttons undone to reveal a chest of peppery grey hair. The shaggy hair on his head and beard echo the same salt-and-pepper theme. Thick lines crinkle around his dark brown eyes.

"Excuse me?" I say.

He grunts with a swing, the wood splitting into two clean halves and the tip of the ax sticking in the log. He rights himself and wipes his brow with the back of his hand.

"Morning. You the new guest?"

"Uh, yeah, I suppose so."

"Atanas." He steps forward and offers the same hand he used to wipe his sweat. I put my fingers into his palm and he shakes firmly. "Thought you'd need some more wood. There's a cold snap coming."

"Thanks, I guess." There's a question to every sentence, but he offers no more explanation. His Bulgarian has a thick accent, but I can't place it. Not that I've spent a lot of time in villages. Or even in this country. Maybe I've forgotten what my language should sound like when twisted by the mouth of an old man.

His arm disappears in the darkness of the cellar, and for a moment I'm taken back to childhood fears of spiders and snakes and all the creatures musty darkness could hold. But he extracts his arm whole, pulling out another block of wood.

"I'm sure we could handle it," I say.

"Nah," he says, plunking the wood down. "Wood's my job."

The darkness of the cellar continues to hold my gaze. I remember jars of jam and tomatoes. Pickled okra and watermelon that was spicy and tangy instead of sweet. But beneath those memories is my pounding heart every time my baba sent me to the maza. Fetch this. Get that. Go into the darkness, you silly child, and stop being afraid of nothing.

He turns, following my gaze. "Haven't gotten around to splitting this summer."

His words break whatever spell I'm under. "I see."

I don't see. I don't understand where he came from or who he is or why he needs to chop the wood this week.

"I'll be finished soon," he assures me, raising the ax to his shoulder. He slings it out and up, then pulls down in a beautiful arc.

I watch him split two more pieces of wood, first in half and then quarters.

"You want to try?"

He extends the ax handle to me, and I realize I've been staring.

"I don't know how," I admit.

"City girl?"

The word girl offends me. I've traveled the world, lived in a foreign country, and bought my own apartment. I'm not a girl. But I don't correct him. Instead, I take the smooth handle he offers. He backs up and leans against the door-jamb, his eyes twinkling.

The ax isn't as heavy as I expect, but it's awkward to heft. I hold it parallel to my shoulder, the way I saw him, then swing.

My arc's too wide, and the blade nicks the corner of the wood, bouncing off and making me jump back as I drop it.

Atanas laughs. His amusement should irritate me, but the sound is rich and welcoming, like he's seen a hundred women throw an ax on their first swing. "Let me help you."

He aligns the piece of wood on the block again, then bends to pick up the ax.

His sweat smells earthy and yet clean. He moves behind me, arms aligning with my own.

"Hold here." He positions my left hand, then right. "And here."

His voice is like chocolate with crisps of cocoa nibs turning it gravelly, and I feel myself responding to him. He seems comfortable being close. Not trying to touch me, but also not afraid of my body. There's no awkwardness in proximity—as if he belongs close to me.

I shake the thought from my head.

"Relax," he says, his voice dropping to the timbre of intimacy.

He lifts the ax. My arms follow the motion, and we swing together. The blade lands halfway down the block of wood.

I grin, but before I can celebrate, he lifts and swings again.

The wood splits with a satisfying crack.

He steps away, and my back is suddenly cold without him.

"You get into a rhythm. It becomes a sort of meditation. Just you and the wood." He takes the ax from my hands and moves back to his spot near the door. "You going to watch me all morning?"

My chest flushes as I realize that's exactly what I want to do. "Would you mind if I did?"

There's a long pause. Most men find my honesty refreshing. But those tend to be Americans from big cities, not an older Bulgarian from a village.

Finally, he laughs. "Nah, girl. I wouldn't mind."

So I watch him.

For the next half hour, he turns his muscles into machinery, splitting the wood in a rhythmic chant. Thud, thud-crack. Pause. Thud. His sharp precision keeps my attention, as does the growing patch of sweat on his chest and beneath his armpits. He's tireless.

When he finally puts the ax down and begins gathering the wood into boxes, I remember myself.

"You must be thirsty. Come in for a glass of water. Maybe some coffee?"

"Sure," he agrees.

He carries one crate, and I carry another. It's heavy and cuts into my thighs with every step. Life outside of cities is so physical. Constant carrying. Breaking. Manipulating. It's not a life I've ever desired, but now it intrigues me.

"You live around here, then?" I ask as I struggle to open the door.

"Yeah," he says.

"Silvena, were you chopping wood?" Philip calls from the kitchen. The whole floor smells of bacon.

Atanas cocks an eyebrow at me.

"That's Phil, my boyfriend."

Philip strolls into the hallway, wiping his hands on his jeans. He takes the box of wood from me and hauls it next to the fireplace, letting it land on the floor with a thump. Atanas sets his down more gently, standing slowly to face Philip.

"Atanas sum. Priyatno mi e."

"Phil."

They shake hands.

"You want breakfast?" Philip asks, breaking eye contact first. His Bulgarian is rough, but understandable.

Atanas smirks, and when he speaks his head turns slightly in my direction. "Sure. Let me just start a fire first."

Atanas kneels in the gaping maw of the fireplace, gray ash coating his knees as he carefully arranges the split wood into a pyramid. While he works, Philip brings in three plates of bacon and eggs, each portion a little smaller than our usual fare. The espresso machine rumbles to life, and he comes in with three coffees.

"Blagodariya Vi za vasha gostopriemstvo," Atanas says, spearing a piece of bacon.

Philip's eyes go wide and he turns to me.

"He says thank you for your hospitality."

"Ivan didn't mention you'd be here," Philip says, messing up both the tense and case. It's almost sweet to see the man who can do everything perfectly struggle through my language.

Atanas pushes eggs around his plate and coughs. "Ivan lives in the city now, too busy to look after the house. I do what I can."

He looks around the room, and his close inspection of the thick coat of dust that has worked its way into the cracks of the decorative molding embarrasses me, as if I'm watching an intimacy I shouldn't be privy to. The light in Atanas' eyes dims, taking them from golden back to nearly black, and if I didn't know better, I would think tears threaten to trace his wrinkles.

I reach out and squeeze his hand. It's just as hot as it was when he was slinging the ax. This man is always on fire.

He offers a weak smile. "You wouldn't believe it now, but this house used to be beautiful."

"I believe," Philip says. "Silvena doesn't you believe. She hates everything about woods."

My draw drops and I glare at Philip. Even in his broken Bulgarian, I can recognize the teasing barb.

He grins back, then winks. Leave it to him to recognize the tightness in my chest and my soft touches for what they are.

"I should get going." Atanas pushes his chair back from the table. "I thank you for your kindness."

He leaves before we can stand, out the door in an instant.

"Strange man," Philip says.

"Shh," I whisper-hiss. "He might hear you."

"So you're into the silver fox?" His tone lilts the way it always does when he recognizes one of my crushes. "Not your usual type."

"There's something about him …"

"Rugged? Strong?"

"Wild."

He scoops the man's untouched food onto our plates, dividing it equally between us. "I can see that."

As the day wears on, I have to tell myself three times to not get distracted.

Remember, I am here playing board games with Philip—learning his strategies and looking into his methodology. Remember, I am here cuddling against him as we stare at the disappointing tangle of woods and talk about our future. Will there be marriage? A child? Perhaps a cat sometime soon. Definitely a cat, at least for me, and can he accept that?

He doesn't like felines, but he thinks the companionship will be good for me. He won't be cleaning the litter box. Or feeding it. Or taking it to the vet.

Remember. I am in the bathtub with my lover's body, tracing the lines of his muscles, softened by our year in Bulgaria. I always thought my country was more rugged, its land rough and demanding. But I've taken a farm boy into the city and made a metropolitan out of him.

"You seem distracted." He runs a soapy washcloth over my skin.

"I'm sorry." I lay my head on his shoulder.

"Thinking about Atanas?"

A bubble of laughter rocks me against him. "No."

"It's okay if you are."

"This week is about us. We can find another playmate when we go back to the city."

He wets my nose. "Not like him."

I pull back. "You like him, too."

He shrugs, a hint of blush creeping into his cheeks. "You're right. There's something about him."

"It's not like anything will come of it," I say.

"Why not?" He rubs from my thigh down to my foot, digging his fingers between my toes until I squirm.

"He's … well, he's not like us."

"How do you know? You think we're the first deviants in the world? The only poly couple alive? People are living like us all over the world … even here."

I lean my head against the edge of the tub, relaxing against his insistent rubbing on my feet. "No, but I know Bulgaria. He's from another generation. And a village."

"Mmm." He stops rubbing, considers. "I've never told you the devious things us farm boys got up to."

I drop a grin in surprise.

"Tell me."

And he does.

CHAPTER THREE

After the bath we make love—that slow, sweet, nearly boring kind that only feels right because it's with Phillip, and then we fall asleep cuddling. Hours later, I wake in that groggy, liminal state between day and night. I roll over in bed, throwing the hot covers off, and let the cool air caress my naked body.

As I lie there, staring at the ceiling, a small noise fills my ears like a high-pitched ringing. I clean out my ear with my pinky, then the other, but the ringing doesn't go away. I press the fleshy part of my ear into the canal. It pops out, but the ringing doesn't stop.

In fact, it grows until it sounds like distant screaming.

Confused, my eyes dart around the room for the source of the noise.

My attention lands on the knot of wood above me. It almost seems to be breathing—expanding—covering more of the thick log. I wrinkle my brow and sit up on my elbows, staring harder at the knot.

It's definitely the face of a woman. The scream grows louder, and I expect Philip to wake, but he doesn't stir.

I lie back, glaring at the screaming knot.

Then, there's silence.

I wait.

Nothing happens.

I stand up on the bed, maneuvering between Philip's feet, and reach up to stroke the knot. It's warm to the touch, hotter towards the center, and in the very center, where the woman's mouth was …

The woman is three-dimensional. She wears a traditional outfit, complete with an embroidered shirt and heavy apron. All that's missing is a coin-studded headpiece. She's a stocky woman, but with a certain beauty about her. It takes me a few moments to recognize the room she's standing in as the living room. There's no dust. The table and bed-turned-sofa are gone, replaced with a low table, a few three-legged stools, and a thick carpet. The woman stands near the fire, which crackles behind her, but it's the dark cloud in front of her that draws my attention.

The woman gasps—a sound between pain and ecstasy—and her white shirt rips, revealing welted skin. Several lines form from neck to waist, blood pooling up and soaking the tattered shirt. The cloud encroaches on the woman, and she moans. Then whimpers. I can barely see her through the dense fog, but more of her clothes are shredded. Her apron drops. Her skirt falls. And through it all, there's so much blood. It swells into beads, then rolls down her skin, pooling below her.

Her whimpering turns to screams. I can see her so clearly that they should be deafening, but they're the same distant ones as before—little more than a high-pitched ringing.

I jerk my hand back and the picture fades instantly.

"Silvena?" Philip says from on the bed. "What're you doing up there?"

My heart's pounding. "I … I thought I heard screaming."

I know it sounds insane, but it's far from the craziest thing Philip has heard me say. He tugs my hand until I fall next to him on the bed.

His voice is low and calm, the way you would talk down a panicked toddler. "Screaming?"

"There was a woman. Phil, I think bad things happened in this house." My eyes dart around the room. The sloped ceiling feels so low, like it's about to crush us.

He wraps his arms around me and kisses my temple. "It's just your imagination. There's no woman. No screaming."

I wait for him to finish—that nothing bad ever happened—but he doesn't. Because he can't know that, and Philip doesn't lie. I shiver. The screaming is still ringing in my ears, as faint as a mosquito buzzing. I stare at the knot, challenging it to morph into a woman again, but it remains a set of concentric rings.

"Help take my mind off it?" I look up to Philip. His strong jaw is set. He hugs me tight.

"You sure?"

"Yes, please."

"Okay. Let me just stoke the fire." He gets up and puts on his sweatpants. He opens the stove, moving around the wood with a poker. The light glows orange on his smooth chest, and I want to run my fingers over the dancing shadows. A pop echoes in the room, and the ringing stops. It's silent, except for the occasional gust of wind against the window.

"Stand up," Philip commands after he closes the stove.

I stand, hands hanging limp at my sides. The fear from what I saw is still sending my heart racing, but there's another thrill rising, competing with it.

"Go to that pillar, there." Philip points to the one nearest me.

I swallow, not wanting to move. He's pointing at the pillar that has an eye-level knot.

"Are you afraid of the knot?"

I nod.

He strokes my bare hip. "Okay, sweetie. The other one."

This time I obey. I move to the second pillar. Standing in front of it, I raise my arms, press my forearms into it, and arch my back, spreading my legs slightly. It's a familiar position, and the anticipation of it slows my fear.

"You ready?" Philip asks.

"Yes, sir," I say.

The first open-handed thwack on my buttocks makes my whole body tense. The fat of my butt jiggles, and the force of his blow sends a ripple of pressure up my sides. Then, the pause. That delicious moment of savoring. My body consists of only the cells his strike has woken. Fear and silly stories of women from a hundred years ago fade. All that exists is my body and the sensations he drives it to.

The second blow comes. The third.

He works faster—smack, smack, smack—until the sound fills the small space. My toes dig into the carpet and my hips try to dance me away from the pain. But Philip is thorough, one strong hand holding my butt in place as the other strikes again.

When my butt is red and the stinging has grown to a steady pulse, Philip reaches beneath me and strokes my pussy. It only takes three long draws of his fingers from clit to ass until I orgasm. There's no teasing or playfulness. It's a service. I fall against the pillar, and he catches me.

"Thank you, sir," I breathe.

He kisses my forehead and scoops me up, carrying me back to bed.

CHAPTER FOUR

The scent of the villa is getting to me. It's not that it smells bad. It's just that musty scent of encroaching decay. It's the way Baba's house smelled in the years after Dyado died. She moved to the first floor, to what used to be a maza and their summer kitchen. She lived alone in those two tiny rooms for fifteen years. When we came for holidays, she would open the main floor for us. We would cook in her kitchen and sleep in every bed available—her house could easily hold the blossoming branches of her family. But it always had the stale scent of disuse.

I hated the way the scent attached to my hair and clothes, like that house was clawing me back to it even after I left.

The smell drives me from the house. Philip offers to come with me, but I tell him I need to clear my head. The low sun shines brightly in the clearing, but I take my jacket anyway, tying it around my waist. My shoes sink into the mud around the house. I do a circle of the clearing, starting at the driveway and working my way around, using a long stick to push bushes back, searching for the hint of a path. Finally, at the back of the house, I find what I'm looking for. Three worn stripes of paint on a tree a few meters into the forest. White, yellow, white. I have no idea where that marking leads, and my phone is no help, still showing the two dashes of no connection. But the destination doesn't matter.

I just want to get away from the house.

I use the stick to beat back the greenery and step over a tangle of branches, water soaking through my jeans. A few steps into the woods and the covering is so tight that bushes can no longer grow. I can easily walk the path, except leaves and debris blends it into the rest of the forest.

I take a few steps, looking for the next white, yellow, white. It's faint on a birch tree. I move towards it. Past it. Keep looking. The treasure hunt for paint markings takes my mind off Baba, which is just what I needed. A distraction. I move slowly through the forest. Every few steps I stop and turn around slowly, making sure I haven't missed the next sign. But the deeper I go, the further apart they are, forcing me to trust my feet to go straight through this unknown land, and the more I trust myself, the more my mind wanders.

I didn't return to Bulgaria for Baba's funeral. I told my parents it was too short notice. She died suddenly, and the funeral was two days later. No time to book a flight and travel halfway across the globe. Even if I could have, the flight would have been too expensive. My parents said that money didn't matter when death was involved—they'd find a way to pay for it—but money always matters.

The truth is, I hadn't seen her since I got sent away.

I stop and draw a deep breath through my nostrils. The forest smells of decay, but in the wild decay is something sweet. Natural. In a house it's the fading of plastics and mothballs—it's all the ways we try to defeat death.

"You, honey, are a Saturday Child." Baba had smacked a deck of cards on the table. "It's time you learned to use your gift."

I was what? Six? Maybe seven. My feet still didn't reach

the floor when I sat in one of her wooden chairs.

"Don't start with that, Mom," my mother said from behind a magazine.

I picked at the edge of a card, moving it from the top of the deck. It flipped over to reveal a naked man and woman standing in front of a mountain. Above them, a winged creature with leaves for hair watched them.

"Is that supposed to be an angel?" I asked, squinting at the shadowy figure in the clouds.

Baba laughed, her deep voice crumpling in her chest and bursting to fill the room. "There is little difference between angels and demons."

"Mom!" my mother protested, this time lowering her magazine. "Don't fill her head with such nonsense!"

I lean against a tree, panting. I can't remember picking up my pace, but I must have. I look around for a tree marking. Squint. Take a few steps. My heart pounds in my chest, whether from exertion or fear, I'm not sure. But there's a hint of paint, just a few steps away and my heart slows. I'm fine. The woods were meant for people like me.

"It's not nonsense," Baba protested. "If you read the Bible, you'd know it's true. What else do you see, Silvena?"

The card was faded and soft beneath my thumb. I bet they were as old as Baba. Maybe even older. "There's a snake."

"Most people miss that." She reached over and pinched my cheek. "But snakes are very important to our mythology. They can bring deceit and pain, but they can also bring help and healing."

The snake was just a green squiggle in the tree behind the woman, the same color as the ground at their feet.

My mother groaned and fully abandoned her magazine.

"Ugh, they're naked."

Now my naked arms prickle in gooseflesh. The forest isn't cold enough to make me put on my jacket, but there's a dampness about it that feels like winter. The tiny hairs on my arms stand on end, as if I've been licked by a cat. Small beads of water form on some of the tips. I'm so focused on them, I barely hear the rustling until it's right behind me and accompanied by a low, throaty growl.

I spin from the tree, falling into a defensive crouch. In front of me, a single wolf growls. Its reddish, matted fur stands on end, and I wonder if it's as scared as me. Or maybe thrilled. I keep my eyes on it and take one step back. It takes a step forward.

From the side, another growl rumbles. I don't take my eye off the first wolf.

"Shh, it's okay," I say.

"They can't understand you, girl." The familiar voice makes my knees buckle. Atanas catches me and sets me on my feet. "I've got you."

It's a code word I use with Philip. It means I'm safe— that I can stop holding everything together. The fear drains from me when I hear it in my own language, as if I'm a little girl and my father is chasing the monsters from beneath my bed. I cower behind Atanas.

He raises his arms high above his head and lets out a roar from his chest. The deep sound fills the spaces between the trees. Even I, knowing the roar is in my defense, sink lower. I lift my eyes just in time to see what looks more like a bear than a man in front of me. He's grown another two feet and is covered in dark brown fur. His mouth lengthens into a muzzle, sharp teeth growing up and down, and spittle flies towards the wolves.

One lets out a whimper, tucks its tail, and flees.

Atanas gives another roar, and the second follows.

When I raise my head fully, he's a man again. Taller than me, yes, and wider too, but just a man.

"Thank you," I whisper.

"You shouldn't be in these woods alone," he chides. "They're dangerous."

As if to emphasize his warning, he collapses.

I catch under his arm and scoot close, the lengths of our sides touching. But his body does not warm me, and he lets most of his weight rest on me.

It's my turn to say, "I've got you."

"I don't come out this far," he says in explanation.

He chops wood for an hour at a time and scares off grown wolves as if they were puppies. I wouldn't think a walk in the woods could tire him. But his skin is pasty beneath his beard, and his usually clear eyes look like the bottom of a puddle.

As we walk, the weight on my shoulder becomes lighter. By the time we press through the bushes back into the clearing, he's walking on his own. His breath grows steady, and we can finally talk.

"Thanks for being there," I say. Which brings to mind, "How did you find me?"

He shrugs. "I've lived in these woods for a long time. I can feel when something's not right."

I'm not sure if he means me being in the woods was wrong or if it was the wolves attacking, but I don't ask.

"Will you come in for some coffee?" I ask.

He looks over his shoulder at the dark woods, then takes a long look at the house. "I'll pass this time."

"But …"

"I need to rest. You go on in. A stiff drink and some rest will do you good, too."

Only then do I notice I'm trembling. I cross my arms in front of my chest and agree to go inside and get warm by the fire.

When I enter, a blast of hot, stuffy air hits me. Philip closes the door behind me as I take off my muddy shoes.

"I was getting worried about you," he says as he unties my jacket from my waist and hangs it on the hooks near the door.

"Worried?"

"You've been gone for four hours. I thought you said a little walk."

"Four hours?" I pad into the living room. Lunch is set out, untouched. "It couldn't have been that long."

But it could have. That forest felt endless.

CHAPTER FIVE

The next morning it isn't chill or imaginary women trapped in knots of wood that wakes me with the sun. It's anticipation. Will the strange wood cutter make another appearance?

Before I gather the courage to emerge from my cocoon of warmth, the thud of chopping comes muted through the closed window. A sleepy smile tightens my lips as my heart catches the rhythm. Its steady forcefulness enchants me, and my hand creeps down my belly, aiming for that sweet spot between my legs. As I shift, the bruises from last night swell with a dull ache.

I stop and roll my eyes. I can't remember the last time I was this taken with the idea of a man. Perhaps not since the raging hormones of high school. I can't even put into words what makes Atanas so attractive. He's tall and thin, skin browned by years of sun. His brown eyes are definitely noteworthy. I usually don't like the brown eyes that have surrounded me since childhood. But his are so rich, almost changing color with his mood, and the crinkles around them hint at wisdom rather than just age. There's something more than just his appearance, though. His strength while chopping? No, not quite …

My hand has started moving again. This time I laugh and throw off the covers. I go to the window and press up on the heavy frame. It slides with a loud creak, and there's a hesitation in the rhythm of the chopping. Then it picks up again. I listen, for just a few moments, then I work up the courage to go outside.

Atanas doesn't miss a stroke as I round the corner, and he doesn't hesitate even when I come near enough that he must see me over the chopping block. He keeps going, emitting a small huff of effort with every down swing. He lets me watch for five minutes before pausing and offering a nod. Then he continues.

I watch him closely, noting the way his grip tightens at the top of his arc and then loosens the instant the blade kisses its target. He grabs pieces of wood from the dark cellar and positions them without fussiness. The wood obeys him, never falling over or shifting beneath his stroke.

"Coffee?" I ask when he finally stops to wipe his brow, as if his sweat is a punctuation mark.

He sets down his ax and takes the cup I offer him. I sip my espresso, which is cold now, but he just stares at his. He runs his thumb around the rim.

"These were made by good hands," he says.

I consider my cup. A tiny air bubble stands out on the milky white paint between the dark blues and greens. "You knew the artist?"

"She lived here a long time ago. Dianna. Like Dionysus. God, could that woman turn a bottle of wine into a party."

I laugh. "I'm afraid we didn't bring any wine. But you'll come in for breakfast again, right?"

Philip has made three portions this morning, loading our guest's extra high. I kiss his cheek as I settle behind my own boiled eggs, ham, and potatoes.

"You need to shave!" I laugh.

"Don't tell me and Atanas you don't like some whiskers on your men," he teases in English.

Atanas cocks an eyebrow at Philip, but doesn't say anything.

Atanas makes his same abrupt exit one breakfast and two coffees later. He thanks us for our hospitality and leaves through the door before we can even say you're welcome. There's a sharp jerk in my chest when he leaves—like I'm missing my chance. But when the door closes, there's only relief. Translating between the two men for an hour has exhausted me.

"I'd almost think we imagined him." Philip lifts Atanas' still-full plate and puts it on his.

"Both of us?" I follow with my plate and cup. "It hardly seems likely."

"Oh, there are documented cases. They call it folie à deux. Or, less romantic, shared delusion disorder. It's when a delusion is so closely shared between two people that it's impossible to tell which one instigated it. Most often among isolated couples." He gestures to the empty kitchen. Leave it to Philip to have a psychological term for the most unlikely event. What I chalk up to ghosts and spirits, he can always explain with science and the intricacies of the mind.

"We've only been here two days." I dump out Atanas' coffee and chase it down the sink with hot water. "Not really enough time to consider ourselves an isolated couple, right?"

"You'd rather you made him up so you can keep him to yourself," he teases.

His words stings as if he slapped me. Sometimes Philip doesn't think. Those months I lost in the hospital, clawing my way back to reality, are fresh in my mind even if they happened a decade ago.

"Nah, I'll share." I think back to the morning, the pink sun burning mist off the mountains as I watched Atanas. "I'd just rather him be real."

"Fine." Philip kisses my cheek and whispers, "He's real."

I stiffen. It's the same way he turned the knots in our room into an audience, coaxing my ripe imagination like a swollen G-spot. But no. Atanas is real. I shake my head and start washing dishes.

"Thanks for dusting in there," I say. "Atanas seemed more comfortable. I almost wonder if he used to live here. The owner's brother, maybe?"

Philip leans against the counter. "You think I had time to dust after getting that thing started?" He points at the still-warm stove.

I stop and return to the living room, soap dripping down my hands. "I swear it's cleaner."

"Maybe you just don't hate it as much." Philip swats my bottom, and I jump. "I'm going to go see about cutting back some of those nettles so we can have a picnic."

"Watch out for snakes."

I return to the sink to finish the dishes, taking special care with each one. Now that I know they're not just some tourist knock-off and come from a local artist, my appreciation for them grows. Their asymmetry and obvious imperfections become, as Philip loves to put it, charming. I'd buy a set if we can find where hers are sold. I'll have to ask Atanas for her phone number.

As I turn over the final plate, I notice an etching on the back. It's faint, and I have to dry the plate and carry it to the window before I can make out what it says,

D. 1908

I nearly drop the plate, then rub at the etching. Maybe it's too worn. 1988? Surely. But that 0 refuses to tighten its waist.

If it wasn't for the plate and the dust, or lack of it, the locked cellar probably wouldn't bother me. But when Philip comes in while I'm on my knees stoking the fire and tells me the picnic's cancelled because he can't get into the wood cellar, my frustration bubbles up.

"Then what were you doing out there?" I ask, sitting back on my heels and throwing my hands in the air. "It's been an hour."

Philip frowns at my overly dramatic response. "Well there are two mazove—"

"Mazi," I correct him sharply. "If you're going to insist on Bulgarian, at least get it right."

He takes a step back, hands up in gentle surrender. "Okay. Mazi. There are two of them. One's half filled with preserves and household items. Stuffed to the brim—you know how it is."

I do know how it is. Bulgarians above a certain age tend to be hoarders. They blame it on the unavailability of anything new during communism, but I swear the layers of junk in most houses date back to before the 1900s. Or maybe everything just feels that old, like we're trapped in a stale time that refuses to move forward.

"I spent a bunch of time looking for a weed eater in there, but no luck. If they have one, it's locked in the wood shed."

"A weed eater?" I frown. "Like, a gas powered trimmer thing?"

He shrugs. "Some are electric."

"You know we mostly use scythes, right?" It might not be true. My entire experience with yard maintenance was a few drunken swipes at some weeds when my friends rented out a villa for graduation.

"Well, if I saw a scythe, don't you think I'd be out there playing death with the bushes?"

I laugh because I can imagine him doing just that, cape and all.

"What's got you so on edge, anyway?"

"I don't know." I pick up one of the larger wedges of wood and plop it on the embers, sending a splash of hot ash into the air. "The maza was open when we came up for breakfast."

"Atanas probably locked it when he left."

"Yeah, but why would he lock that one and not the other? Why would he lock it at all?" I lower a second log across the top, and the first one shifts down in the embers. "It's not like someone is going to come all the way out here to steal wood."

"Maybe that's where he keeps his tools."

I don't like the idea of not knowing what's lurking in the darkness beneath our feet, and locked rooms have always made me uncomfortable. Too many secrets held with rusty keys. But I can't make Philip understand that irrational fear. He'll chide me like I'm still a child afraid of the dark. And he'll be right to do so. Too many days I still feel like the child my baba used to send down to the cellar to get a jar of tomatoes or her spicy pickled watermelon. How I'd whine and twist and refuse and … in the end, still be forced to go.

"There's just something off about him. Why didn't Ivan mention he'd be here? And this morning—" I let my voice fade.

"What happened this morning?"

He's going to think my mind is acting up again. Maybe it is. "He said he knows the woman who made the plates and cups. You know, the blue and green ones."

"Those are great," he says. "If he knows the artist, maybe he can introduce us."

"That's what I thought, too. But, when I was washing them, I saw a date. They were made in 1908."

"1908? Then you must have misunderstood."

I roll the conversation over in my head. My memory has always been shit, but the conversation, which should be fresh, is shrouded in a particularly thick fog. What exactly did he say? He knew her? Maybe he had heard of her.

"Maybe you're right," I sigh.

Philip kneels next to me. "Let's worry less about the caretaker and more about your complete inability to build a decent fire."

I frown at the scattered embers and two logs that refuse to catch flame. "Teach me, oh great fire god."

"Okay, city girl. A fire needs three things: fuel," he holds up one of the split logs I've been trying to arrange, "heat," he points to the lighter by my knee, "and oxygen." He runs a thumb over my lips, traces it down my chin, and though his hand falls from my skin, the thrill of it skitters all the way to my nipples.

"How do you do that?" I whisper.

"Do what?" He holds my gaze.

"Make me feel so powerful."

He smiles. "We all have our gifts."

We spend the next fifteen minutes building a log cabin that Philip assures me will allow air flow and direct the smoke up instead of into the room. When we're done, he opens a damper by pulling a metal cord next to the chimney, which pulls air through the structure and coaxes the flames to life.

I want to call the beauty magic, but I bite my tongue. Philip wouldn't like his knowledge reduced by my superstitions.

After, we go for a walk. I long for a classic wooded path, but after yesterday, I don't dare.

"Did you know there's wolves in these woods?" I say as I watch the fire grow.

"Really? I didn't realize."

"Bears too."

He laughs. "Maybe we'll see one today."

I laugh too, but only then realize I haven't told him about the wolves yesterday. Why on earth would I not tell him? Even now, my jaw won't unlock so I can let him know what I went through.

"Maybe an eco path?" he suggests.

There's probably one nearby, harboring waterfalls and rope bridges, but with no internet, it will be impossible to find. My mind spirals, kicking myself for not doing more research on this place before we came. I could have pinned a few spots, found the nearest monastery, and been prepared for the complete isolation of the cabin. Instead of complaining again, I allow Philip to lead me down the road, edged in to a single lane by the aggressive foliage.

"Was the road this bad when we came?" I ask as we walk

hand-in-hand in the middle of the street.

"Yeah," he runs a hand over the branches. "If you paid any attention while I drive, you would've noticed."

Either the fresh air, the exertion, or the distance from the house lifts my spirits, because I don't bite at his bait. We make it all the way to the narrow wooden bridge that had me white-knuckled on our drive up.

"See?" Philip points to the rusted steel strips supporting the worn beams. "I told you there was nothing to worry about. That bridge is built to withstand centuries of abuse. Our little car was fine."

We step onto the worn wood, which is as solid as he says. He rubs the small of my back as we lean on the railing. Even now, in the calm of the bubbling brook and chirping birds, I can't help but imagine a speeding car rounding the bend and plowing into us. Everything about this bridge—this life—screeches, "Precarious."

I turn and kiss Philip, slow and lingering. I force myself to close my eyes and concentrate on the wet of his tongue as it oscillates between soft and firm. When I pull away, his breath smells of bacon and coffee, and the woods smell of sweet autumn decay.

Philip pushes my hair back and stares into my eyes, un-blinking. "Nothing to worry about."

He gives a lock of hair a quick tug, pulling a sharp laugh from my lips like a puppeteer. In moments like these, I'm happy to let him be my puppet master.

The bushes at the mouth of the driveway seem to have grown even closer during our excursion, and pushing through them is like a reverse birth, returning to the womb we share with the dilapidated house. The warm, sticky air trapped in the breezeless clearing completes the effect.

"I think it will rain again," Philip comments.

Gray clouds have snuck across the sky while we were gone, sealing our bubble of land in a pregnant weight.

"We can cuddle through the storm," I say.

"Apparently with a bottle of wine." Philip lifts a dusty bottle from the porch. The dirt crusted around the edges betrays years in a cellar but at least it's glass instead of the plastic two-liter bottles most people use. If it's well-corked, it might be drinkable.

After dinner and two rounds of rummy that neither of us are into, we take Atanas' gift to bed. The liquid that pours out is dark as blood and smells of warm spices beneath woody flowers. It attacks my tongue with a sharp, coppery bite then eases into a flood of flavor that continues to roll through my mouth after I've swallowed.

With the first sip, I'm thinking of Dianna. She could turn a bottle of wine into a party. What had Atanas expected us to do with his present? Were we supposed to save it and share it with him? Have a party of three?

I lower my nose to my glass, and now the earthy notes smell familiar—like Atanas behind me, wet with sweat. The fat raindrops now falling on the roof sound vaguely of wood being chopped.

Lightning flashes, stunning my vision, and a sharp crack of thunder follows. I jump, almost spilling my wine, and Philip laughs at me.

"Come here, baby." He opens his arms. "I've got you."

I scoot into his embrace and pull the covers over us. After the bright flash, the room seems even darker. The open stairwell is inky black.

"Could you close the door?" I ask. "And draw the curtains?"

"Still feeling watched?" He gets out of bed, and I ball my hands into fists as he approaches the open door. He closes it softly. Thunder claps in protest as he yanks the curtains into place, as if the sky doesn't want to be shut out.

I shrug, eyeing the knots carefully. But tonight they refuse to transform into women.

"The wine is delicious," I say more to the room than to Philip.

He clinks his glass against mine, then sets it next to the bottle. "You enjoy that. I've got my own drink."

With some maneuvering, we get my pants off, and his head falls eagerly between my legs. The wine tastes even sweeter with his tongue warm on my clit, and my apprehensions fade to ecstasy.

CHAPTER SIX

The electricity of the storm is divisive. Instead of drawing together for body heat and comfort, we're irritated at each other's closeness, seeking solitude beneath separate chunks of comforter. The storm grows throughout the night, pelting the roof so hard that a few insistent drips come through in one corner. Philip and I have a stare-down over who will find a bucket, and he finally tosses off the blankets, making sure to uncover me as well. I allow myself to suffer with him, not covering back up until he's in bed. But then he falls asleep immediately while the inconsistent plop, plop of the drip keeps me up.

Hours pass, and I draw the blanket tighter around me. The air grows colder, and I know I should get up to stoke the fire, but every time I move, my eyes fall on the wooden beams between me and the stove.

The women are back. There's no mistaking the knots for random circles, and there's no missing the pain in their twisted faces. Their breath comes out from the darkest, innermost ring, which has turned to a hole in three of the knots. It crystallizes along the woodgrain before disappearing. The screaming returns—and the fire's out this time, so it can't be water escaping the wood.

I curl my fingers around the edge of the blanket and try to shut out the sound. It can't be real. Just the settling of the house and howling of the wind. But when I close my eyes, I still see the room as vibrantly as if my eyes are open. A woman is sitting on the bed, weeping. She wears a checked dress with a belt, and her hair is done in a neat braid. She has the neat, carefully ironed appearance that was valued in my baba's time. A man in dress slacks kneels in front of her.

"The house," she cries. "There's a ghost."

The man caresses her cheek. "There's no-one here."

"We can't live here. Please."

"There's nowhere else for us to go. That your father gave us this house is a miracle."

"But …"

"You'll get used to it," the man promises. "You'll see."

"Can't you feel it? It's so cold."

The man embraces the woman. "Let me go get some wood."

My eyes fly open. The scene was crisp in my imagination. The people real enough to touch. I stare at the sad woman in the knot across from me—the one that wished she was me but wanted to look away. The wood holds her in place, and she couldn't look away even as I came in front of her.

I blush, hot with shame.

"I'm sorry," I whisper to the cold night.

I must fall asleep, because the next thing I know, the room is warm enough that my feet try to sneak out from under the covers. I moan and stretch and reach out for Philip, but he's not there. My hand searches the empty bed, as if I might find him tucked away in the folds of the sheet. I roll over to look at the time. Nearly eight, but the storm's still going, and it has blocked all hints of daylight. Wind shakes the house, alternating between a low moan and a whistle.

Last night's vision comes back to me, and I sit up with a jolt.

"Phil?" I call.

As if cued, he returns with an armful of wood. The cavity of the stove devours it, and he strikes a match to light the fire.

"Get dressed and come down," he says, his tone that of a child at Christmas, not excited for his own gifts but for his parents to open the macaroni-art he made in school.

He disappears where he came from. I pull on pajama pants, a hoodie, and socks, then follow to see what he's up to.

The door to the living room's closed. I try to open it, but it sticks. With a little weight it pops open and I tumble awkwardly into the room. Atanas and Philip stare at me from the table. I pull my hoodie lower over my pants, wishing I had put on actual clothes.

The room is warm enough for me to loosen my clamped muscles. A cheerful fire crackles in the fireplace, and the table is set with three plates piled with eggs and bacon. In the center of the table sits a golden loaf of freshly baked bread. I stare at the round loaf. Not bread. Pitka. It smells of traditions that can't be translated, and the small dishes of honey and colorful salt standing sentry next to it demand I respect its name.

"You made breakfast?" I ask, assessing Atanas in a new light. He's nothing like the older Bulgarian men I've met, who depend solely on conserves when a woman isn't around to cook for them.

Maybe it's just the flames, but I swear the tops of Atanas' cheeks turn a reddish-pink.

"I made breakfast," Philip says. "Atanas brought the bread."

"That storm's something fierce. I stopped by to see if you needed anything."

"And you brought pitka?"

"You two have been so nice to me. I wanted to show my gratitude."

"It looks pretty. Thank you, Atanas." Philip says in his broken Bulgarian. He tears a large chunk from the bread. It comes off easy in his hand.

I sit, but still hesitate with the pitka. I recognize the shape and way it breaks. I know the chosen condiments in a way Philip doesn't. It's the welcome pitka, given to guests. Not something you bring into another's home. The coffee is from a djezve, which means burnt, thick, and strong enough to tip a migraine, but I sip it anyway. The coffee and bread take me back in time, and I can see the three of us sitting on stools around a much lower table. The image of the screaming woman being torn to shreds flashes in my mind and I bite my lip to still my heart.

After two swallows I force myself to break the bread. Up close, it isn't as perfect as it first looked. The crust is crisp and nearly snaps, but the inside is soft and still warm. It's probably the only pitka the man knows how to make. That a man his age bakes at all is impressive. Besides, it's not as if this is our home. Philip and I are just guests.

The dark honey sticks to the crevices. Atanas watches me closely as I raise it to my mouth and take a bite. The bread crumbles and the honey oozes, smearing my mouth. The three of us laugh.

"Atanas, you live here. Tell me, storms common?" Philip's stilted Bulgarian tightens my chest in shame. His wisdom disappears in his fight against the language. Except he doesn't seem to be struggling. He's easy in his ignorance, throwing words that don't quite fit with the confidence of an orator. There's a boldness to him that I still can't find in English even after living in the US for years.

"Not common, no. But they happen. And they hit some places harder than others," Atanas says gruffly.

Looking around the room, I have to agree. It would be so easy to lose power, and with no phone, the place would be complete cut off from society. But who even lives in these woods anymore? Old men and women, forgotten by their families. People who hardly leave their homes even when the weather's fine.

After a drawn out meal, Atanas stands to make his usual exit, but Philip is quick to cut between him and the door. The two men nearly collide, and Philip puts his hand on Atanas' bicep.

The two men stand close together, with Philip' fingers curled around Atanas' thin shirt, and my stomach lurches in response. Philip towers over me, but Atanas is even taller than him. Seeing the man I usually think of as my protector dwarfed excites me in unexpected ways.

"Stay." Philip's pronunciation is off, but the softness of his gaze says things his vocabulary never could.

"You're sure?" Atanas asks. His eyes don't leave Philips face, but the question twists around to me.

"Yes, please," I answer. "The weather's terrible, and there's no reason for you to go out in it. Stay here."

He nods, but pushes past Philip, out of the room, and I'm afraid he's disappeared again. He returns a minute later, holding two bottles of different sizes. The dirt caked on them betray the same wine he left yesterday.

"Were you planning for this?" I ask with a laugh.

Atanas shrugs. "Most situations can use a bottle of wine."

"Let's go upstairs, where we can relax more," Philips says. We leave the dishes on the table, taking only the wine, cups, and our selves.

"This is delicious," I say when the first sip passes my lips. It's an echo of my words yesterday, and suddenly I feel the same sensation of being watched. But now Atanas is here, and I can see his eyes on me, and being watched is not such a bad thing. I pace a slow circle around the room, caressing the wood paneling and running a finger along the armchair.

Atanas settles on the rug with his legs tucked to one side, a grown man set up like a little girl at a sleepover. Not wanting to tower over him, I join him on the floor. Philip sits beside me, our backs against the bed. Atanas leans against one of the wood pillars, his head just beneath one of the screaming women. I keep my gaze focused on the man instead of the imaginary women above him.

"Wine is the soul of the earth. Best drank close to its source."

"Wine is ..." Philip's brows furrow in concentration. "The soul of ..."

"The earth," I fill in the rest.

Philip raises his cup in cheers. "You and Silvena will get along well. She believes in souls and superstitions." He's given up speaking Bulgarian, but Atanas nods along as if he understands. "She's a subotnika."

"Saturday's child?" Atanas turns to me, eyes aflame with amusement. His accent curls around the title in a way Philip's doesn't, breathing life into the word. "I should have known. You have the spark about you. An affinity for spirits. Protection from evil. Blessed be, Saturday's child. Do you hunt vampires, like in the tales?"

His excitement is from another generation—like that of my grandmother when she tied a red thread around my wrist and told me I was meant for great things. People my age don't even know what a subotnika is.

"No vampires," I say with a laugh. "I just have a healthy respect for the possible."

"The possible and most often, the unproven parts of it," Phillip teases.

I roll my eyes, wishing he would switch back to Bulgarian so I wouldn't have to translate when he mocks me. But Atanas doesn't seem to mind the English.

"Then maybe just searching for spirits." Atanas winks at me. "Most of them washed away with the cynicism of modern times, but the hills and trees around here give our spirits something to cling onto."

"Tell us a story about the spirits, Atanas." Philip sweeps his arm across the room, opening a space for Atanas' tale. I raise my eyebrow, shocked at his interest. Whenever I talk about ghosts or spirits, he reminds me that entertaining such fantasies isn't good for my condition and changes the topic as quickly as possible.

Philip shrugs. "How else will we pass the time?"

My hand resting on Philip's thigh, I can think of a dozen other ways we can pass the time, but I can't imagine initiating any of them until we finish at least one glass of wine.

Atanas looks from me to Philip and back again.

"He would like a story," I say.

Atanas closes his eyes, softening his wrinkles until they're almost invisible. Serenity washes over his face. He opens his eyes to a silent expectation. The moment stretches out before he finally nods. Then he's on his feet and rapping his knuckles on one of the wooden pillars. He hits just above one of the women, and I shudder for her. It almost seems like the knot opens wider, her silent scream growing.

"I'll tell you about the domavik of this house."

I swallow and can feel the blood draining from my face. I can handle a story about this mountain or even the nearest village. I'm not ready for a story about this house.

"Go ahead, girl. Tell your boyfriend what a domavik is."

I take a deep gulp of the wine to steady myself, then look at the thick carpet. "Well, I don't know exactly. The domavik is an old concept, even I don't know a lot about them. They're from the Slavic times, I think?"

I glance at Atanas for help, but he's just staring at me, waiting. I paw at the carpet, separating out strands. "It's like the spirit butler or protector of the house. He lives in …" my mouth drops open, "the woodshed. V mazata za durvo?"

"Mmm," Atanas clicks his tongue. "You're confusing the domavik with the stopan, maybe."

No, I'm not confusing the two. I would never confuse anything with a stopan. I remember clearly meeting my first stopan when I was a child. Nine years old, the summer was hot as hell, one of those still years when time seemed to stop. And there were snakes everywhere, laying in the shadows, slithering through the smallest puddles of water. They were aggressive that year, even the ones that usually slithered away at the sight of humans were prone to lash out when crossed. The boys of my village chased us with the creatures, pinning the snakes' necks in their small palms and releasing them in the middle of our games of cats cradle so we would run away, shrieking.

One afternoon Baba sent me down to the maza for a jar of jam. As usual, I refused. But she insisted, and I could never resist her mulberry jam. In that dark, cool space, half-filled with chopped wood and half with preserves, a long snake slithered from beneath a shelf, moving over my sandaled foot. Unlike the others, it was calm. Slow. Without thinking, I reached down and picked it up.

The creature curled around my arm, moving up and squeezing against me.

I grinned, the stupid child that I was, and thought I would finally have my revenge on the boys.

I took the snake into the yard, through the garden, towards the large tree my friends played under. The oldest boy looked up, saw me standing like a woman on a crucifix, the snake winding around my arm towards my neck. His eyes went wide, and instead of laughing or shrieking, he whispered, "Silvena, put it down."

I looked at the snake's head, inches from mine. It was more colorful than the ones the boys found, with a thick swirl of black waving down its back. It flicked a red tongue at me from a cutely upturned nose. I smiled back at it.

The cluster of children backed away slowly, terror in their eyes.

I frowned and lowered my arm, edging the snake off me with my free hand.

"What?" I asked.

"Get away from it," the older boy commanded.

Later, I told my Baba about the viper. Her eyes didn't go wide, and she didn't yell at me, like I expected.

"You're gifted, child," she told me. "The stopan doesn't show himself to just anyone."

The weight of that responsibility still coils around my

heart, squeezing until I can't breathe at times.

I glare at Atanas. "Some stories say they're the same thing, the stopan is Bulgarian and usually takes the form of a snake. The domavik fills the same roll, but in the form of a man."

He snorts. "Hardly. But go on. What do you think a domavik does?"

I think back to the books I've read, their faded images of witches and samodivas burned into my mind. The one my baba gave me for my twelfth birthday, along with a pack of tarot cards that my mother hated, had a line or two about the domavik. "He's sort of the spiritual head of the house. Usually a dead ancestor? He watches over the people who live there. If they take good care of the house and behave properly, he keeps them safe from sickness and other calamities. If they disrespect him, he could make them ill or even kill them." This time I don't bother translating to English, and Philip's the one leaning towards me, trying to catch the meaning of my words.

Atanas stretches up, resting his palms against the top beam and arching his back. He seems to have grown, filling the space.

"Such a basic description. What are they teaching children these days?"

Philip laughs and wraps an arm around me. A finger traces the bare skin of my neck. "So then, tell us the truth."

I take another gulp of wine. My glass is half-gone and I haven't been able to enjoy the thick spice of the drink. But it's doing its job, calming my racing mind. I settle against Philip and ease into his slowly wandering touch.

"The domavik is not an ancestor of the family. There's no hint of humanity in him. And he's not the head of the house, but its heart. When wood is chopped from a forest to build a home, the spirit of the forest, or part of it, remains in the logs. For months, sometimes years, the spirit is trapped in that dying wood. Imagine that—going from roaming an entire forest to being trapped in a few logs, cut off from the rest of your spirit and all of your power. As the sap dries, the spirit leeches into the home. Of course it wants to protect the house—all it has left for a body. Protecting the people inside," he shrugs and lowers his hands, "that's just a consequence of them living there."

"What do you mean? I always heard the domavik was a loyal spirit."

Atanas laughs, low and gravelly. Philip's hand has inched below the collar of my shirt. His fingertips move in slow, soft circles over my breastplate.

"Loyal." Atanas smiles, his face contorting in the low light. "Does this sound like loyalty? A domavik would sit on a person's head while they slept, smothering them. In their dreams, they would see the spirit and, if they kept their wits about them, they would ask, 'good or evil?' Do you know what the domavik would answer, more often than not?"

Philip pinches my nipple just hard enough to make me gasp. "Evil."

"But who knows if the domavik was talking about himself or the men who cut down his forest and built their homes with his carcass?" A shadow passes over Atanas' face, and my hand twitches with the desire to reach out and smooth it away.

I sit up a little, moving away from Philip's warmth. "You really think this house has a domavik?"

Atanas caresses the wood at the same tempo that Philip

caresses the underside of my breast, curling his palm around the curve. "It's an old house, its bones were built over a century ago with wood from this clearing. Of course it has a domavik. But you two don't seem bothered by him."

Philip grins. I've melted into his lap, no pretense at sitting properly. He waves Atanas closer. "Why don't you sit with us?"

Atanas kneels in front of us, then shifts his weight, sitting near my head, which rests on Philip's thigh. At my neck, I can feel Philip getting hard. He removes his hand from the stretched collar and works at the edge of my hoodie, pulling it up slowly, dragging the fabric over my belly, waiting at my breasts. He gives the shirt a final tug and my breasts pop into the open, jiggling at the quick motion.

Atanas licks his lips, as Philip fondles first one nipple, then the other, forcing them to stand at attention for our guest.

"Silvena's quite the woman," Philip says. His hand leaves my nipples, traces down my belly, and disappears beneath my pants. I wriggle into his touch, my hips begging for more. "And so sensitive."

"It seems like the lady could use another drink," Atanas says. He lifts my glass from the floor and puts it to his lips. He draws a swallow into his mouth, then leans over. His eyes are sparkling blue as they come near. Then his lips are on mine, and he's releasing sanguine liquid into my mouth. I pull it into me like a kitten at a teat as Philip fills my pussy with his fingers. Philip presses deep into me, holding me in an arch, and I moan against Atanas' mouth, seeking his tongue now that the wine is gone.

The man's hands are on my torso, his grip harder than

Philips, but slow and confident as he finds my breast.

My head swims with the wine and the man feeding it to me. His beard feels like pine needles brushing my face as I walk through the forest. Philip works me faster, and I'm overcome with the sensation of running through the woods, feeling the cool air on my bare skin. Atanas surrounds me like a warm mist blowing down from the mountains.

I shudder and try to close my eyes, but they're already closed. This forest, the cave I stand next to, and the mist rushing from it aren't real. They're only in my mind.

My eyes fly open as my body spasms with orgasm.

"Mmm, good girl," Philip says, easing out of me. Atanas pulls away as well, and I'm left panting between them.

"That was …" I murmur.

Philip nods. "We saw. You looked like you were having a very good time. What say we lose some clothes?"

He's speaking English, but we've gotten to the point where our encounter no longer needs shared language. We've had threesomes with men from other countries. Ones that neither of us understood. After the first orgasm, it's easy to forget Google Translate even exists. He takes off his shirt, and Atanas follows, unbuttoning to reveal a toned chest with springy hair.

Philip reaches across me to take Atanas' open shirt and moves it down his arms, twisting the fabric in his hands to hold the man in place.

Atanas looks down at Philip's hands, but speaks to me. "I've never done this with another man."

Philip leans forward, pulling the shirt, but giving Atanas space and time. I hold my breath. Finally, the older man leans in and brushes lips with my boyfriend. Their touch is soft, barely meeting. Nothing like the deep exploration we shared, and I wonder if it's enough to make Philip taste pine and see the wilderness. When they break, Philip smiles. "Don't worry, we've got you."

They give me space to sit up, and the three of us sit in a bare-chested triangle. Philip and I both take our wine glasses and sip. Mine finishes, and I glare at the bottle across the room.

"You don't drink?" Philip nods to Atanas' still full glass next to the wooden pillar.

"I've got enough wine in here." Atanas pats his chest.

I stand and stretch, then walk to Atanas' glass. I lift it and take a sip. Enjoying the eyes of both men on me, I stretch again, this time bending over and pulling my pants into a puddle around my feet. I step out of them and face the pillar. I settle my weight on my forearms, arch my back, spread my legs, and wait for whatever they might do to me.

Fingertips brush my ankle, and I'm not sure whose they are until the springy chest hair caresses my buttocks. Lips kiss my hip, and the hand moves up my leg. Philip reaches around from the other side of the pillar and guides my hands further up, giving him room to duck in front of me so I can lean on the familiarity of his chest. I grip the wood behind his neck as I feel the warmth of a strange cock trace my wetness.

I close my eyes, breathing heavy. Philip kisses me, his lips soft and warm. "Open your eyes."

I comply. His face has that pure joy it gets when we start to play. "Do you want him?"

I can feel Philip's arm moving beneath my breasts as he slowly strokes himself.

"Yes."

Philip kisses my forehead, and I can only imagine the

look the men exchange before the cock teasing at my opening slides into me.

After the initial spreading, he thrusts into me hard, like an animal, and I squeal, but hold firm against him. Philip laughs and holds my hips steady.

As he hits a rhythm, I'm returned to the forest. My feet fall with his thrusts, left when he's at my G-spot, I rock with him and right when he's just about to leave me. The trees are so old and the world is so quiet, and all that's here is me and this fog that surrounds me. Atanas' hands grip the fold of my hips and he pulls me onto my toes. The fog pins me against a tree. *Thrust.* A rock. *Thrust.* Against the strain of sunshine on a summer day. The man behind me is forgotten. It is only the fog thrusting into me, and I feel years pass in each thrust. The movement is like the growing of tree rings. Inevitable and unstopping and so fucking consistent. My skin spreads in concentric circles. Ripples. I'm losing skin and self.

I moan into Philip, who allows me collapse into him. Atanas removes his cock, and I'm cold in the reality of the room, despite the popping stove only feet away from us. I straighten my wobbly legs and move close to Philip, letting his chest and thighs support me.

"Let's move her to the bed," Philip says, but his voice is far away. I cling to his shoulders and let him sweep me up against his warmth. My eyes flutter open. There is the face I know and trust. My eyes circle the room and find Atanas, cock still at attention as he stands at the edge of the bed. His member looks smaller than it felt in me. For such an average man, he filled me completely.

"You doing alright?" Philip asks, laughter in his throat.

"So good," I murmur.

"Mmm, I thought so." He places me on the bed, and no sooner does he release me than both men move onto either side of me, pressing my body between theirs. Their hands roam my skin. I search for lips and find Atanas' eager to cover mine. His tongue grows thick in my mouth, unwinding and pressing into every crevice. I want it to move through my entire body. I open my mouth wider and arch my neck to swallow more.

I'm no longer on the bed, but lying on a rock, sun kissing my exposed flank. A brown snake with a black line of paint down its back slithers towards me, and I open my mouth to it. It moves slowly, centimeter by cold centimeter, to fill my mouth. My jaw widens more than I knew it could, and the serpent wriggles deeper into my throat. I'm vaguely aware of Atanas' whiskers brushing my cheeks and his fingernails, permanently stained by a life of work, tracing slow, soft circles around my nipples. I'm even less aware of Philip easing his cock into my pussy, splitting a body that doesn't matter when I exist in sunshine and forest. The snake eases into my belly. I moan around Atanas' tongue, and his laughter vibrates me to my core. His hands move down my stomach, to my dripping pussy. I squirm on the rock. The snake in my mouth is so still. I merely breathe around it, feeling the slightest pulse of its scales. It tastes of iron and summer. Philip removes his familiar cock from my pussy, making room for another snake. This one comes in faster, springing as if caught lazing beneath a rock. A distant thought of venom worries at my mind, but then I feel Philip behind me, spreading my ass. He would never let me be poisoned. The snakes push into me from top and bottom, throbbing with every millimeter of movement, and the mist drops down again, heavy and thick. When Philip enters me, my entire body shudders with a chill.

The mist holds every memory of the forest. Every footstep. The laughter of lovers discovering each other in a shadowy hollow. Then the distant sound of ax against wood. Its sharp blade pierces the skin of a tree. The ax falls with the rhythm of my men, like the rolling of a train. The mist grows thicker until I'm the tree, my skin turning to bark.

I cry out as they strike.

It hurts, but Philip holds me. The pain is sweet, and the sap that runs like blood tastes of ancient candy.

I'm not sure if I scream or moan. Branches tremble around me and I'm holding on by a few fibers and then I'm falling into blackness.

CHAPTER SEVEN

I wake up to the timeless half-dark this house seems to live in. With the clouds still hugging the clearing it could be late afternoon or the middle of the night. If it wasn't for the two men lying on either side of me and the pounding of a hangover, I would think our late-morning romp was a dream. I wiggle to the bottom of the bed and pad to the bathroom to relieve my bladder. My body aches in all the good ways, everything swollen and dusted in a few sweet bruises.

After peeing, I run the bath, not bothering to be quiet. Whoever wakes can join me. But neither man stirs. I dip into the hot water, my used muscles relaxing in the warmth, and try to piece together our encounter.

I lost track of how many times they made me orgasm. The pleasure ran together with a certain amount of pain. Not real life pain, but that damned forest that I couldn't get out of my mind. I can still smell its summer pine beneath my finger nails. I soap a washcloth and scrub at them. Sniffing again and again until I only smell lavender cream.

By the time the water cools the only movement on the bed has been the two men absorbing my space, leaving me no room to crawl between them. I dress—real clothes today—and head downstairs.

The fire is long dead, and there are only a few pieces of wood in the basket. Somehow, we've used the entire line of wood beneath the bench. I draw out the decision to fetch more wood by making and drinking a coffee. But by the time I finish the espresso, I'm shivering. Someone needs to go for wood, and I'm the only one awake. I throw on my jacket—too light for this weather—and open the door to a thin dribble of rain.

"Going somewhere?" a voice asks behind me.

I startle, then relax, flooded with relief. "We need more wood."

"I'll get it," Atanas says, moving close behind me. He presses up against me and closes the door. "You don't need to go outside in this weather."

"It's no problem," I say, even though the last thing I want is to go out in the rain. No. The last thing I want is to go near that cellar.

"You don't like the maza," he says, reading my mind.

I shake my head, staring at the worn wood grain of the door. "I don't know how to explain it. But it's just … this place where things go to die. Memories get shoved into them until they're bursting, and then we close the door and lock them. And no one ever sees what we put away."

I'm surprised at the words dripping from my mouth. They're admissions I haven't even shared with Philip, but they come out easier in Bulgarian. Maybe because they were put there in my native language— the months I was locked away in what felt like a cellar, tended by women who spoke in short, terse commands and the therapist who taught me the only way to get out of that place was to bottle my emotions like pickled conserves, and stack them neatly on the shelves of my darkest hollows.

Atanas wraps an arm around my waist, cradling my stomach, and his lips brush my neck. "You let me get the wood. That's my job."

I turn around and find his lips. His kiss is different. Almost hesitant. And there's no mist or forest. Perhaps it wasn't his kiss that drove me there and just too much wine.

After a moment, he pulls away. "Your boyfriend doesn't mind if we're alone?"

His voice sounds different when I don't have to think about translating. It's a language I can fall into—words that can cradle me. I rub my forehead on his chest. "No. He doesn't mind."

"Then, come with me." He leads me into the living room and, with a single motion, pushes the table away from the couch, butting it up against the far wall.

The room is so cold that I shiver, but his touch is like tiny flames on my skin. He doesn't undress me completely, but pulls our pants down just enough to rub against me. This time, I'm careful to keep my eyes open as our hips grind together. He bites his lower lip in pleasure, moving slow and steady outside of me, with none of the urgency of the night before.

His cock moves from the fold of my thigh to my pussy. "Can I have you, Silvena?"

The question is thick and feels archaic. Almost ritualistic. I shiver. "Yes."

He moves inside and all sense of chill leaves me. I'm a burning log on a fire. I'm a burning bush spouting commandments. I'm all things that have ever burned in the wilderness. And I'm his. His breath falls on my cheek like oxygen on fire, flaming me hotter.

The ecstasy of slow burning is more exquisite than any sexual encounter I've had before. Years of playing at BDSM, being tied up or whipped, used and humiliated, doesn't compare to the vulnerability of being consumed by an undying ember.

As much as the idea of possession usually repulses me, with this strange man, it entices me.

"I'm yours," I murmur, the words surprising me as they slip from my tongue.

"Yes," he answers.

I want it to last forever.

As if my thought pushes him over the edge, he finishes and stops moving. His weight collapses over me.

"It can," he says.

"What?" I murmur.

"Last forever." He pulls out of me and I am suddenly blanketed with cold.

I wipe myself with a napkin from the table and pull up my pants.

"I'll go get the wood," he says.

When he leaves, I lean back against the tapestry. The wood creaks behind me.

"The spirit lies." The words hum against my back.

I sit up and sweep the tapestry to the side. Beneath it is a large, burnt umber knot, twisted in swirls and rotting in the center. It looks nothing like a face, but the woman's voice pours out of it.

"He promises forever. But we're not spirits. He can't make us like him."

A whisper of screams echoes beneath the words. I touch the edges of the knot.

"And when he fails, he leaves us here to rot."

The front door slams, and the knot falls silent. I let the tapestry drop over it as Atanas comes in with a box of wood.

"Let me get a fire going for you," he says. "Can't just

keep warming you from the inside."

My stomach jumps at his hint, and I want nothing more than him keeping me warm from the inside again. Now and forever.

There's that damned word again. Forever. Something I never feel with a stranger—something Philip has been coaxing out of me for years. And this man dances with the word as if he can't be extracted from the concept of time.

The fire crackles to life and Atanas turns to face me. His eyes dart to the tapestry, then back to my face. "You look like something's bothering you."

I shake my head. "No, I'm fine."

"You're sure? I don't want to overstep my bounds. This, with your boyfriend, is new to me."

"Philip," I remind him.

"Yes, Philip. I'm just not used to sharing."

"Not many people are." My defenses melt at his honesty. "It can be a little awkward at first. But you liked it? Last night?"

He looks out the window. The storm has cleared and a gentle red light fills the horizon—I'm not sure if it's sunrise or sunset at this point, but he figures it out quickly enough. "You mean this morning?"

I laugh. "Time does funny things in this place."

"That it does, girl," Atanas agrees. He pats his jeans. "I'm going to fill you guys with wood—actual wood, no metaphors—then I'm going to get going."

"You don't have to," I say, not sure if I mean he doesn't have to get the wood or doesn't have to go.

"I want to make sure you're warm tonight. The storm brought a cold snap, and there's no sense in either of you going out. Fifteen minutes, and I'll have you set."

Atanas lines the wall with logs again, then leaves. When he's gone, I go upstairs to find Philip. He's groggy, but sitting up in bed, and beckons me to him.

"Where you been?"

"Downstairs talking to Atanas."

"You fuck him?" Philip kisses my hairline. "You dirty girl."

I laugh away a blush and snuggle under the blanket, still dressed.

"So he gets you naked and I don't?" Philip fakes a pout.

I don't bother explaining that Atanas got me with my pants pulled down a foot, but get out of bed and undress. The sheets feel better against my naked skin anyway, and there's something comforting in Philip's familiar warmth.

"Can I ask you something?"

"You just did."

I groan and smack his chest. "I'm serious. Do you think Atanas might not be what he seems?"

Philip squeezes me. "What do you mean? Who do you think he is?"

My voice grows tiny in my chest and has a difficult time pushing past my lips. "Not who. What. You don't think he could be a domavik, do you?"

Philip snorts with laughter. "No, I don't. Because I know they don't exist. The question is whether you think he's one."

"He's so strange. He just shows up. No car. No path to his house that I can find. Where the hell does he come from?"

Philip holds me tighter and lowers his voice. "Maybe he's the boogeyman, living in the maza, waiting to eat your toes."

"I'm serious! The owner didn't say anything about him, but he's here all the time. You don't think that's strange?"

Philip's embrace loosens and he sighs heavily. "I shouldn't have let him tell that story. It was too much for you, wasn't it?"

"No," I protest. "It's not the story. I want to explain the visions I had while we were fucking, but at this point it will probably make things worse.

"Are you feeling guilty about what we did?"

I stiffen. "No. Why?"

"It's just, you do this." He kisses my hair again, but this time it feels more patronizing than sweet. "After we fuck someone you come up with some absurd reason why he's weird or dangerous."

"I do not." I wriggle free from his arms and lay staring at the ceiling.

"What about the Russian guy we met at that rave?"

"The one that had a gun?"

He inhales deeply as if steadying himself to explain something to a child. "It was a kink. And it wasn't loaded."

"You didn't know that at the time."

"And at the time, you seemed excited about it. You weren't worried until we got home. And then you literally burned his number. That's what I'm talking about. In the moment you're down for anything. Then afterwards, you find all these reasons to never see our partners again."

"So you wanted to see him again?"

He groans. "This isn't about him. It's about you."

"Right. Me."

I turn my back to him. For a moment, I think he'll turn and spoon me and we'll talk things through. I'll agree that I'm overreacting and he'll be sorry he had to point it out again. But he turns the other way, just our butts touching.

He can't be asleep already, and I'm not tired, but we lie there, not moving. In the stillness, I hear that damned screaming, back to the faint hiss of water escaping from wood on the fire. I close my eyes and see only knots on the back of my eyelids. Their edges glow, as if they're burning from the inside.

In my mind, I see another woman in the living room. Her thick, long hair is loose, and she's completely naked. The same fog is descending on her, and her flesh is melting away. She screams and tries to hold her skin to her body, but everywhere she touches, more sloughs off. More and more until only bones are left. The bones clatter into a pile on the floor, and the fog condenses over them, turning into the shape of a man. I snap my eyes open before his features come into focus.

Something horrible happened in this house. More than once. I'm sure of it.

I stumble from the bed to the window and yank against the wood, but it doesn't budge. I pull again, then flap my hand around the top, searching for a latch. Nothing. I push against it, frantic now. It's like being in that cell. They called it a room. Two meters by two meters, a bed and a chair and a window that wouldn't open. They called me lucky—some rooms had no window panes and the winter wind blew in without mercy. Even my window was a pane of sugared ice that radiated a chill into the room. I caught pneumonia twice in the four months they kept me. I press harder, my palms

turning purple. I hiccup, not sure if I'm coughing or sob-
bing.

Strong arms wrap around me, slowly pinning my hands
against my chest.

"Hey, hey, shh. It's okay."

"It won't open," I say, stupid tears filling my eyes.

"I've got it." Philip releases me and moves to the window. He struggles, but gets it open a few inches. "There."

I gulp the cold, wet air that soars through the small gap,
and Philip puts his hand on my back.

"I'm sorry," he says. "I didn't mean to be so harsh."

I straighten and slow my breathing.

"Tell me what's wrong. This isn't about Atanas, is it?"

I bite my lip.

"Come on, you can tell me."

"I … I hear screaming," I say. "And I see these women
who were … I don't even know how to explain it. But something bad happened here."

"That sounds horrible." He sighs heavily. "But Silvena,
you realize this is your mind playing tricks on you. You
know these things aren't real."

"I know. But they feel so real. I see them." I shake my
head, trying to clear my mind. I look up at Philip—the man
I've trusted for so long—but his face is blurry through my
tears. The wood-woman's warning comes back to me. "I
hear them."

He hugs me again. "Do you want me to help you?"

I bite my lip, then nod.

"Okay. Can you get undressed?"

"Yes."

"Yes?"

"Yes, sir."

With that, our contract is complete.

I slip out of my clothes, fold them with shaky hands, and lay them on the bed. Then I wait for a command. He positions me against the pillar, this time with my back to it, exposing my face and breasts to him. It won't be an easy session. I keep my head down. There's a certain numbness at the edge of my brain, but my fear still swirls in the center.

"Are you sure you want this?" Philip asks.

I nod.

"Say it," he commands.

"Please," I say, finally raising my eyes to meet his. "Help me forget."

"Get on your knees."

The first blow comes like fire across my cheek. It hits like a needle on my bone, then spreads like blood leaking from a murder scene, warm on my cheek, my ears, my neck. My whole body turns hot, and I want to shed not only my clothes, but my skin.

"It's your imagination."

I close my eyes, feeling the real sting, tasting the real blood.

Yes. It's my imagination.

He jerks me to my feet and pushes me against the pillar. His flat hand is heavy on my chest.

I thrill at the fast motion as he pins me against the wood. I try not to think about the way Atanas had me pinned last night. This is the important moment—the one I need to hold onto and sink into.

Philip presses on me, adding more weight until the room goes gray and my hands go cold.

"This is real," Philip assures me. "I am real. You are real."

He releases, and I collapse against the pillar. Blood rushes to my head and my body begins to shake in orgasm.

Through the rolling, he gingerly strokes my cheek, raising my face so my eyes meet his.

"Thank you," I gasp.

The scene continues, and I fall deeper into Philip's definition of reality—one that is accepted. One that feels safe. One that is real.

After, he holds me while I cry.

"You're okay," he coos to me. "I've got you."

"I just don't know why my mind comes up with these things."

"It's not your fault, Silvena. You were raised with people who constantly told you that you were special. The adults you trusted called you Saturday's child—a woman who could see spirits. They expected impossible things from you. That would mess with anyone's mind."

I nod and snuggle into his sweater. He's wrapped a blanket around me. "It just feels so real sometimes."

"I'm here to remind you it's not. Any time you need."

CHAPTER EIGHT

The next morning is the first time all week that I wake up with a clear head, sure of the time and my position in the world. I stretch and give a kitten yawn. My eyes flutter open to the most beautiful sight: soft sunshine streaming through the window. The clouds have finally lifted.

I knead at Philip's calves with my toes until he turns around and captures me, pulling me to him.

"Feeling better?" he asks.

"So much better," I say. "Maybe we can go for a hike today."

He assesses the window. "It's probably muddy as hell."

I give a disappointed "awww."

"But we'll at least get out of bed," he says. "Maybe we can drive into town. Get some more food and see the sights."

"I think the sights are three crumbling buildings and maybe a graveyard somewhere."

"Then that's what we'll see."

On our way out of the bedroom, I caress the pillar I had been pinned against yesterday. I find one of the knots and trace its shape. Nothing like a face.

On the first floor, Philip stops to make a coffee. "Just coffee? We'll get breakfast in town."

"You keep saying town. I don't think it can even be considered a village."

He smacks my bottom. "Then we'll go further. We've got a car and all day."

Through the closed window, I hear the steady chop, chop of the ax, and my stomach tightens. Maybe Philip's right and I'm feeling guilty. As natural as our open relationship feels, it goes against everything society has taught me since birth.

"Let's say hi before we leave," Philip says, downing the end of his coffee.

I finish mine, and we put on our shoes. But when I try to open the door, it sticks.

I check the lock, sliding the bolt back and forth. I pull harder, and it pops open. I fall back against Philip and he catches me.

"Did that always stick?" I ask.

"Storms can make wood swell," he tells me, setting me on my feet. "Like the window last night. Shall we?"

We step onto the porch and are greeted with a mess of a yard below us. Patches of dark wet have soaked through the weeds, puddles of mud bubbling up.

"Potential for a slip'n'slide," I note.

Philip grins. "Or mud wrestling."

We pick our way around the corner slowly, careful not to fall. Philip keeps his hand on my elbow to steady me.

This time Atanas stops quickly. He holds his hand out to catch a beam of sunshine. His sleeves are rolled up, forearms bare in the warm morning. "I thought you two might sleep all day. Wouldn't blame you after yesterday's … activities."

"First good weather in days," Philip says in English,

miming a steering wheel. "We thought we'd go for a drive."

Atanas' smile falls for just a second. "That sounds nice. You two enjoy."

The brief flash of hurt sends an ache through my chest, and I release my grip on Philip's arm to lean in for a hug. Atanas hesitates, then wraps his arms around me. In his loose embrace, I smell sap and turned soil. I inhale deeply and hear birds. A squirrel chitters. Somewhere a wolf cries at the moon, and I want to stay in his arms, listening to that song forever.

"We'll be back in the afternoon," I promise.

I let Philip turn me back towards the car, but when I do, I see two clear sets of footprints in the mud. Mine and Philip's.

When we get in the car, Philip laughs.

"What?"

"You didn't ask to peek in his mysterious cellar."

"I didn't," I agree. The thought hadn't even crossed my mind despite Atanas standing in front of the dark opening. Let him have his secrets, and let him keep them locked far away from me. "Let's get going. I'm hungry."

Philip puts the car in drive and eases into the messy brush of the driveway. I crane my neck, looking back at Atanas and the two sets of footprints. They aren't melting into the mud. Then we're into the trees and I can't see the house, let alone the mud.

Philip drives slowly on the road, avoiding downed branches and thick sludge. It's almost as if we're walking again, and the slow rolling of the wheels, sticky on the soiled pavement, irritates me.

"Can't you go faster?"

"Not if you want to actually get to town," Philip says. He

slows down even more.

When we turn the next corner, my irritation spasms to fear.

"What's that?" I lean forward in the seat to look at the tangled mass of branches reaching across the road.

Despite our slow speed, Philip slams on the brakes, and we stop well back from the downed tree.

"Well damn." Philip gets out of the car and I follow him.

The crown of the tree, laid directly in front of the bridge, bushes out almost twice my height.

"There's no way we're moving this," Philip says. "We're going to have to wait until someone comes and gets rid of it. Who even does that in Bulgaria? Road services? Emergency services?"

My mouth hangs open and I shrug. "How am I supposed to know?"

I reach out and touch a branch. It's only been down a day at most, and it still feels very much alive. I wonder for how long after a tree is cut it still holds that wet possibility of life.

As I wrap my hand around a branch, the world shifts. The tree tilts until it's standing and I'm beneath it, looking up at the sun through its branches. Wind blows and takes me further into the forest. The trees grow around me like a labyrinth tightening around a lost wanderer. I'm back at the clearing, but the house isn't there. I'm surrounded by trees, freshly cut, being planed down to square logs by several men. I feel each peel of bark come off my skin. Blood drips from my skinned flesh, pooling on the grass beneath me as dark as mud.

I gasp and jump back. But the peeling continues. Deeper. Insistent.

"Sil?"

My name comes to me from the forest. I turn to try to find it. Philip has his arms around me.

"Silvena. What's wrong?"

His embrace hurts on my raw skin, but the sensation fades, and I'm standing next to the fallen tree, unable to explain what just happened.

"Nothing," I say.

"Does your phone get reception here?"

I go to the car and pull out my purse. No bars. "Nope."

"I guess we go back. Atanas probably has a phone at his place. Or maybe he can help move the tree, if it comes to that."

I nod. "I guess so."

"But when we go back, no more of this women in the walls and Atanas is a spirit stuff. He's a kind man who happens to live alone in the woods. He's a bit odd, as one can expect from someone so far removed from the flow of modern society. But he's not a domavik, because domaviks aren't real. Okay?"

I bite my lower lip and look up at the blue sky.

"Baby, even if they were real, do you think one would take the form of a wood cutter and have a threesome with passing city folk? As far as I know, that's not what spirits do."

He knows nothing of spirits. His experience is limited to bible tales of ghosts and angels. Nothing that would dip into the darkness of sex and depravity of desire. He wasn't raised on the stories of vampires and his teenage years were not filled with erotic novels about succubi. He doesn't even watch horror, so he has no idea just how entwined the spiritual and sexual are for most people. I'm not alone in this.

But I nod.

"You'll be nice to him?"

"Wasn't I nice this morning?" I pout.

"You were." He leans and whispers in my ear. "Like a very good girl."

<hr>

"You forget something?" Atanas calls when we park.

Philip looks at me pointedly over the car. I try not to slam the door and call back, "No. A tree's down in the road."

"Really?" Atanas turns the corner, his shirt unbuttoned enough to reveal his chest.

"Yeah. Just before the bridge. It's a big one, no way around it. Do you happen to have a phone we could use to call emergency services?"

He wipes his hands on his pants. "Yeah, I can call them for you. But I can't promise how quickly they'll get out here. That was a pretty rough storm. There's probably some damage all over the region, and this road hasn't ever been their priority."

"Of course," I say, smiling sweetly. "But we can find some way to amuse ourselves until they get here."

A smile spreads over his face, and for a moment there's the warmth of a second sun beaming at me.

"I'll go make that call for you. I'll come back later today and let you know what they say."

"We don't want to be any trouble," Philip says. "I could come with you."

"Nah. No sense in you trekking all the way to my house. Stay here. There's more wine in the kitchen, if you'd like."

I'm careful to watch him go this time. He leaves through

the brush in the driveway and turns right, up the road where we haven't explored yet. Perfectly reasonable.

"You feeling any better?" Philip asks.

I toe at the mud. Our footprints are still there from the morning. But try as I might, I can't make out a third set of footprints in the mess. "I'd have felt better if you went with him."

"C'mon Silvena. He's obviously just a lonely man."

"You're right," I agree.

But as soon as I step into the house, the wood is hissing warnings at me.

"Can we turn down the fires?"

Philip laughs. "Not sure there's a knob on them, but yeah, we can let them die down a little. You hot?" He pulls at the hem of my shirt. "I could help you get out of these clothes."

I swat at his hand. "Don't you hear the hissing? I think the wood's still wet."

"Seemed dry to me. But you have better hearing. Why don't you grab the wine, sit, and peel a couple of tomatoes for a salad? I'll fry up some sausage."

"Okay."

I sit at the table and Philip washes the bottle of wine, opens it, and pours a tall glass for me. He then washes a bowl of tomatoes and puts them in front of me with a small paring knife. I start with the easier of the two tasks, lifting the wine to my lips.

I inhale deeply and hesitate before drinking. Every time I drink, I'm taken to the forest. Maybe it's nothing about spirits. Maybe the wine is just off. Not corked properly and some bacteria has gotten in. Can bad wine cause hallucinations? But it smells warm and comforting, and neither of the men seem to have any issues with it. I take a long draw, close my eyes, and let it work its magic. Not the forest-spirit kind, but the alcohol-spirit kind.

When my nerves are steady, I open my eyes and pick up a hefty tomato. I run the back of the knife along its thick skin, loosening it from the flesh. Then I poke the top of the tomato and peel the skin away. Juice drips down my fingers into my palms. It plunks into the bowl with thick drops. I'm reminded of being flayed on the lawn.

Deep breath. It was all just my imagination. Philip says so. I listen for his movement in the kitchen. The bang of a pan. The sounds of scraping and frying. Normal sounds.

I continue peeling, taking breaks to sip the wine, getting the glass wet with tomato juice and dripping seeds on the table cloth. By the time Philip comes in, the table looks like a miniature massacre.

"Always so elegant with the tomatoes," he says, shaking his head. He puts the frying pan on a cutting board and sets an onion next to me.

I peel the onion, and tears sting my eyes as I slice it into the mush of tomato.

A knock at the door makes me wipe the tears away, which just makes everything worse. Philip laughs at my wet, messy situation, kisses the top of my head, and lets Atanas in.

"You missed me so much you were crying?" Atanas teases.

I roll my eyes. "Onions."

We sit down to lunch, and things are easier than I expected. Atanas says a truck should be out to remove the tree the day after tomorrow. I look at him with his rolled-up sleeves as he loads his plate with meat and salad and decide he is definitely a man.

A charming man.

Who I liked yesterday.

I take another sip of wine, which drains the glass.

"You want another?" Philip's eyebrows furrow in concern, and I know he's not asking about the wine, but if I want to fuck Atanas again, because another glass and I'll get horny.

"Sure, why not," I say. He fills my glass and then leans over and kisses me full on the mouth.

"Proud of you," he whispers as he leans back.

For his part, Philip keeps the conversation going through lunch, asking about Atanas' past and current life in the woods. He struggles through the Bulgarian, not asking me to translate, and I sit back, listening to them. My language sounds strange coming from both of them—an American who can't twist the sounds his ears never heard as an infant, and the old man who drops letters as if he's gotten bored with them from a lifetime of use.

They're both doing the work, trying to set me at ease, and they're successful. I look at the man across the table and feel a tug in my belly. None of the fear I had the night before. If there's any out-of-place sound, it's birdsong and the whisper of wind through young oak. No screaming. No warnings.

"I've been here alone for so many years that I sometimes forget what it's like to be around other people," Atanas admits as he spears a piece of sausage. He points around the room with his fork.

"But there are other renters, right? And the owner. Ivan?" I say.

"Mm." He nods. "Most of the renters are young couples,

like you. Except they're completely wrapped up in themselves. No time for an old man like me."

"You're not that old." Philip puts his hand on Atanas' bicep and the men share an extended stare. I bite my lip with thinly veiled pleasure.

"Either way, you folk have been kind. I don't just mean yesterday, though that was fun. But the meals. The coffee in the morning. It reminds me what it was like to have people living here, not just passing through."

"I get that," I say. "When I first moved to the states, it felt like everyone was rushing along on these lifelines that I couldn't quite see. And because I didn't have one, I was invisible to them."

Philip looks at me like he can't understand me. I'm about to translate when he hugs me to him and whispers, "You were never invisible to me."

"What about you, Philip?" Atanas asks.

"Him? Phil's not been lonely a day in his life."

I remember the way he commanded a room in university. Everyone listened to his opinion on economics. Sociology. History. Whatever he happened to be talking about. They shouldn't have cared about the opinion of a small-town boy, but they listened. Me? I could barely get a sentence into the room before someone was stepping on it with the next topic.

I blamed my language for my slow formulation of ideas. I blamed my limited knowledge, being from a small country. But I knew more about European affairs than any of my classmates. The truth was, attention was something that had to be demanded, and I wasn't any good at asking for it.

"Men are often more lonely than they let on," Atanas says. I'm almost jealous of the attention he's paying to Philip at the moment. I scoot closer to my boyfriend, just to be in his line of sight.

"Did you have a wife?" Philip asks. "Children who come visit?"

"A wife, yes." He looks around the room and sighs heavily. "They called her Kiki. The kids, when they were here, were hers. Never mine, not really. But then that's how things were."

That now-familiar stab of unease hits me. He's talking about this house. He's seeing his wife and children in this room.

I gulp the wine.

"It doesn't have to be that way," Philip says. "Times have changed."

"Some things are too far past to change." Atanas stands and traces the edge of wood where the wall turns to white-washed plaster. "But you two are different. Something I've never known before. Do you often share lovers?"

"Often might be an overstatement," Philip says.

I realize he's switched to English, but the men seem to understand each other perfectly fine. Lubricated by wine, they seem to feel each other's intentions as easily as they did in the bedroom.

"Maybe once or twice a year," I say.

"And ... you don't get jealous?"

Philip and I exchange a not-so-secret smile. "No. Not usually. I think it helps that we usually play together. And there are no secrets."

"What a life that must be. No secrets."

"Well, no secrets about that," Philip says.

I stiffen against him. "Then what secrets?"

"You know, there's always some privacy. It's healthy."

My heart flips in my chest. "I thought we told each other

everything."

"Sure, everything important. I'm just … like you don't care about what I had for lunch last week."

I move away from him. "I wouldn't call that a secret though."

"You're right." He smooths my hair back. "Not a secret. Bad choice of words."

"But you said …"

He pulls me to him and kisses me, silencing my protest. I muffle against his lips, then soften. "You see, the thing about Silvena is she latches onto ideas and her brilliant mind just runs away with them. Consequence of being so smart, I think."

I flush and pull away from him, not sure if my embarrassment is at the compliment or the implication beneath it.

"Just last night she was going on about you being a … what did you call it? A domavik?"

Philip laughs and raises his glass to Atanas, and for a moment I wish a hole would open and swallow me.

"Is that so?" Atanas' attention finally shifts to me. "And you weren't afraid?"

"Oh, she was afraid," Philip says. "But she's come to her senses. Haven't you, baby?"

He pulls me close to him and I let him, my limbs weak over his betrayal.

"I just …" I open and close my mouth, trying to think of an acceptable way to explain away the accusation that someone is a ghost.

"You tell a good story," Philip fills in for me. "I can respect that."

Atanas reaches across the table and pats my hand, which has gone numb. His touch is hot, and warmth spreads up my arm.

"What about now?" he asks.

"I'm fine," I say, which doesn't answer any of the questions swirling between us.

"Maybe I should go."

Philip hugs me, and I'm still weirdly limp in his embrace. "Yeah, maybe that's best."

Atanas bows his head to each of us, then stands to leave.

"No," I say. "Don't go."

He turns, his eyes hungry as they take in my face. "No?"

"I wasn't afraid yesterday. Not when we were together." As I'm saying it, I'm realizing it's true. I'm also realizing that at the moment I don't want to be alone with Philip, who so carelessly flays my weaknesses for strangers.

I scoot out of my boyfriend's arms and stand, embracing Atanas. He wraps his arms slowly around my waist, one hand creeping low on my buttocks. I can feel Philip staring, and for the first time I don't want to turn him on. I want to make him angry. I don't look back at him. Instead, I stand on my tiptoes and press into a gentle kiss.

Antanas' breath flows into me like a stream warmed in the summer sun. I breathe him, our lips melding slowly. I let my tongue creep soft into his mouth. He tastes of moss on wet rocks and the freedom of bare skin.

I moan, not having to fake it, although in that moment I would.

When we break, I lean back and whisper. "You, sir, take my breath away."

I feel Philip tense at my use of the word sir. It's not that I've never used it on another man in front of him. But he's usually there, next to the man, absorbing some of my worship. Today, I determine, it's not for him.

"Why don't we go upstairs," Philip says gruffly, standing behind me.

Things have shifted. Even with Philip at my back, kissing my neck, I'm more alone with Atanas than I was yesterday morning in the living room. There's something about actively shutting out Philip that isolates us. I build slow kisses with Atanas, falling soft into his mouth and chest. He allows me to explore him. If he's aware of the battle between me and Philip, he doesn't let on. He just pulls me close.

It's Philip who removes my shirt and unbuttons Atanas' so we're chest to chest. It's Philip pushing me gently to my knees before the man, as if apologizing by letting me worship another. He unbuttons Atanas' pants and pulls out his cock, stroking it lightly as he kneels behind me, letting me sit on his thighs.

He doesn't issue a command. He knows that today, he's not my sir, and that he knows is delicious. I lean back against him, his chest still clothed in his soft sweater. It's a nudge of forgiveness. He wraps his arms around me, squeezes me, then releases.

I look up, and Atanas is waiting, staring down at us with his ancient brown eyes.

I take his cock in my mouth.

It tastes like wet wood. Young and freshly cut. I run my tongue down its length, feeling grooves that twist like the grain of wood. I swallow as much of him as I can, and my nostrils are assaulted with the scent of a sapling. I groan around him, his flesh vibrating against my hard palate.

"Good girl," Philip encourages me, but his voice is far

away. I'm lost in a blue sky. Milky white clouds puff by, and when Atanas blinks, there's a moment of eclipse that has me squirm further onto him, sucking him down as far as possible.

"You taste …" I gasp between licks. "Divine."

He rubs my cheek like a deity blessing a worshiper, then curls his hand around my neck and pulls me forcefully onto him. I gag, then relax and spring forward, rocking my head against his hand.

Philip is all kisses on my back and short, terse whispers of, "Yes, yes, suck him."

But Atanas is silent. Staring. His enjoyment is stoic, only the slight flutter of his eyes when he cums in my mouth. The hot fluid tastes of sticky nectar, waiting to be made into honey wine. I swallow, then lean back on Philip's thighs. Philip holds me, and Atanas descends to our level. He kisses me, probing the last hints of spring that he exploded into me.

The three of us move to the bed, switching places effortlessly. I lean against Atanas' bare chest, arching my head to continue kissing him. While his kisses transport my mind to spring forests, Philip works my body. I respond to my boyfriend out of habit, arching at the right time to send us both rolling into ecstasy. But my mind is on Atanas' kisses. They are rolling and deep and endless.

"Divine." I breathe again, each time he lets me up for air. He smiles, sometimes laughs, then covers my mouth again.

I hold his cock in my hand, feeling it stiffen and relax through the peaks and ebbing of my own orgasms. Philip drives me to the edge over and over again, pushing me off, then bringing me back up. He works me to screaming with his hand, and when I am exhausted and melting into Atanas, he moves his cock into me, pushing me even further. I lose all sense of space and time, sandwiched between my boyfriend and the divine.

Finally, the three of us collapse together, exhausted.

Philip falls asleep immediately, but I slither out of bed to wash.

Atanas follows.

"Come with me," he whispers.

He takes me down the stairs, and I follow him on tiptoe like a teen that might be caught sneaking out.

When we get to the living room, he spins me into him and kisses me. Enveloped in his naked embrace, my exhaustion gives way to excitement.

"I want you," he says.

"Again?" I laugh.

He pulls away and stares at me. "As my wife."

This time my laugh is high and nervous. "Your wife?"

"I've been alone here too long. I need someone by my side."

The fire is just red embers, and I move closer to it to warm my naked body, and to put some space between me and this man. "I can't be your wife. I'm with Philip."

"He hurts you." Atanas' voice is deep and close behind me. "He hits you."

"That's … not everyone understands. But he only does that when I ask him to. It helps me." The fire pops, like the back of a hand against a cheek.

"It helps you forget who you are. The things you see and feel. Your power."

I shake my head. "No. It helps me keep things straight. Wait! You were watching us!"

He clucks his tongue softly. "Don't play, Subotnika, you

know what I am."

My body turns to ice despite the fire in front of me.

"No," I whisper. "I don't."

He places his hands on my shoulders, and warmth radiates from them, spreading into me.

"You do."

My jaw clenches. "Spirits aren't real."

He spins me to face him. I don't want to look, but we're so close, there's nowhere for my gaze to rest except his face, which seems older. Wiser. A little blurry around the edges. And inhumanly gorgeous.

"Divine." My breath catches in my throat, and the word comes out as a half-sob.

"Not quite," he smiles, fading closer to the man I know. But a bit of the shine stays in his skin. "Just a domavik."

I can't believe this. It's my imagination. If I give in to the delusion, I'm lost. "I should go upstairs."

"Silvena." His voice is gentle, not teasing like Philip's is when he chides me. "I want you by my side. Forever. My new Kiki."

I swallow and let him wrap an arm around me and pull him back against his skin.

"Kiki. Your wife … Kikimora?" I say.

"Yes." His voice rumbles against me.

"I'm …" I want to say I'm not like him—not a spirit—but I can't bring my lips to say what he is. "Philip and I are a pair."

"You didn't feel like a pair tonight." He nuzzles his beard against my forehead.

"That wasn't fair of me. I was … I used you. To get back at him. But … we are … I—"

Atanas silences me with a kiss. His tongue grows, extending into my throat, widening my esophagus as he pushes into my stomach. I can't breathe, but I don't need to. He's filling me with air. Oxygen so pure it burns my lungs. My head goes dizzy, and he pulls back. I gag and sigh at the same time, then cough.

The fire pops and a spark lands on a knot of wood, burning an unsymmetrical ring in it. I wait for a whisper or distant scream, but there's only the continuing crackle of the fire.

"You've done this before, haven't you?" I ask.

His eyes turn stormy and distant. He caresses the wooden beam above the fireplace. "This house is almost two hundred years old, and it's been empty for a hundred of those. Kiki left when the family moved away. She followed her children. Her grandchildren. Their bloodlines. But I don't have that option. As long as this wood stands, I'm bound to this place."

I step back, but run into the lip of the fireplace, almost stumbling into the embers. He reaches out and steadies me, keeping his warm hands on my biceps.

"I can give you endless pleasure. Unbelievable knowledge. Just stay with me."

I keep staring at the knot on the wall. No woman forms, and no whispers call to me.

"Philip ..."

"When I first met the two of you, I felt a certain possibility between us. I thought things would finally work because of the way you share. Maybe this would be something you could share, too. You're right that I've tried this before, and I've learned most women, even the strong ones, cannot hold the power of a domavik. But the more you're here, I realize it's not the strength of you as a couple. It's your ability I'm feeling, Silvena. You can be my wife, and I can give you eternity."

"I've never wanted eternity," I admit. If anything, my one human life has sometimes felt too long, stretched thin for years.

He cups my chin and raises my face to look at him, saying nothing.

I bite my lip and push forward, leaning my head against his chest. "Will you show me the real you?"

"Then you will agree to stay?"

"How can I know until I see you?"

He steps back and my skin feels cold without his touch.

His eyes close, but I still feel his gaze on me. I stare as his naked body blurs. The hair covering his muscly thighs shivers like a spider in ecstasy before spinning web. I inhale, noticing my own body vibrating in response. He exhales, as if my breath is his own. Then his skin splits, not down neat lines, but along atoms, slowly expanding into a cloud that hovers around his core—not blood and bones, but something dark and wet.

Terror echoes through me. All the screaming comes back, not from the walls, but from somewhere inside me. This is what tore them apart. This is what flayed their skin and exposed their souls.

Despite every part of me resisting, I reach into the mist, ignoring the burning of my fingers, the tingling of my arm.

The cloud continues to expand, like a storm covering the horizon. It encompasses me, and the room becomes black.

No, something darker than black.

It becomes abyss.

I can't breathe. I'm a child paralyzed by the darkness at

the edge of my bed. I can't move. I'm a teen with my first boyfriend, unable to say yes or no. Or anything. I can't exist. I'm in the dorm, at a party, frozen in fear. I'm locked in a room. The syringe plunging me into a stupor.

There's a pulse. Like my mother coming in from her room. Like my best friend telling me it's okay. A thicker pulse, echoing to my core, like the first time Philip took my hand.

The pulse grows and the sensation shatters.

Atanas stands before me, the playful smile gone from his lips. His eyes are serious and expectant.

"That was … intense."

"That was merely the edge of what I can show you. When you're mine, I will be able to share experiences stretching back to the beginning of time. I was born when the first seeds sprouted on desolate ground, and I hold its memories like blood pumping through me."

I reach out, but my hand hesitates before touching his forearm. "That must be lonely."

"You cannot comprehend the loneliness of nature." He steps forward, closing the space between us. I don't take my hand back, and his arm moves into it, until I'm grasping at his skin which, despite everything I've seen, feels like flesh. His mouth covers mine.

For the first time, I'm not taken to the forest. Or to my own past. We stay in the room as he lifts me and pins me against the wall, my buttocks pressed to the recently singed knot. As he enters me, he's fully man.

"Don't close your eyes," he commands. He sounds like Philip. Demanding. But also knowing what's best.

I keep my eyes on his face, his wrinkles deepening as

effort flushes him. The moment feels more real than anything I've felt since we've reached the house.

I grunt with him. We groan together. When he cums, I'm a second behind, and he lets me slide down the wall as I'm still rolling in ecstasy.

"You'll stay," he says, looking down at me as I sit on the low bench.

"I need to talk to Philip …"

He shakes his head. "He won't understand. You know he never understands spiritual things."

Unable to control my head, I nod.

He turns to wipe himself with the dishcloth, and my head falls to the side. The knot is hissing again, as if it's been on fire this whole time.

"I … please … I need some time."

"I can't force you. You have to agree." He throws the soiled cloth on the table. "But please, say yes. Soon. I need you."

Then he's gone. Like all the times he's left, except this time I'm certain he's just disappeared.

CHAPTER NINE

Too many hours spent in bed, not enough movement, and another storm blotting out the sun has made me lose track of day and night again. For most people it's a goal of vacation—let go of time completely, and you'll no longer feel the stress of obligation or responsibility. But I'm far from anything that can be called relaxed. At some point Philip stretches, doing yoga and calisthenics to wake himself up, then returns to bed, lounging across it, somehow taking up both sides. I can't bring myself to get in beside him. The house is too still, and Atanas could materialize from any splinter of wood.

More frightening than the thought of him listening to everything and showing up whenever he wants, is that I want him to. I crave the experience of his touch. I want to inhale him and learn his history. And I can't stop my mind from racing after him.

While Philip sleeps, I wander the room, listening to every creak for a whisper that might be Atanas. I caress the wood as if it's his body and wonder if he can feel me. But he doesn't materialize.

I near the knots, sometimes whispering, sometimes screaming, but always a buzzing just beyond this plane. Swallowing my unease I run my finger around one, like the open mouth of a lover. I can feel it turn to flesh beneath my fingertip. But not the smooth, soft flesh of women's lips. It's bumpy. Rough. It sloughs off and a chip of wood hits the floor.

I jump back as the splinter bounces on the carpet.

Then I approach again. I squat, so I'm eye level with the knot.

"Listen," it hisses. But it's not a hiss. It's a distant scream. I push my ear closer to the knot.

Philip stirs in his sleep, mumbling something. I straighten and smooth my sweatshirt over my stomach.

This is ridiculous. Philip is right. There are no spirits. No monsters in the forest. It's my own mind playing tricks on me. Atanas is just a man with an imagination as vivid as my own.

Still, I don't return to bed. Instead I slowly reach my hand back to the knot.

"What did he do to you?"

I caress the edges of the wood again, my finger drawn to the center as if being sucked by a tiny whirlpool. I let it edge closer. Closer.

Then, zip. The wood closes tight around my finger.

I squeak and pull back, but I'm stuck in a vice that tightens the more I pull.

"Phil," I try to scream, but it comes out as the same whisper-hiss I've been hearing all week. I feel as flat as the women I've been pitying.

My knuckle cracks, and I stop trying to jerk my hand free.

"Please," I whisper, this time to the wood. "Let me go."

But it holds me, squeezing tighter until a numb tingling spreads up my arm.

"This place is cute," a woman's voice says from behind

me.

"Well, you definitely got us away from the city," a man agrees, his voice flat.

I spin as much as I can, looking over my shoulder, but there's nothing there.

"We'll have a good time," she says. "You need a break."

"You need me to take a break," he grumbles.

My finger is pulsing, blood unsure of where to go. I bite my lip as the tingle turns to pain.

"Ivan's not bad, not really. He's just under a lot of pressure."

"He hits you." This time I recognize the voice as Atanas'.

"Only when I get in his way."

"You don't deserve that. No woman does."

Her voice is thick with hurt and, running beneath it, the familiar vein of pumping desire. "Like a forest doesn't deserve to be chopped down."

My finger is turning purple. The pain has gone silent, and behind me I hear the grunting and moaning of furtive lovemaking.

"I heard you with him. The fucking woodcutter."

"You don't understand. He's not ..."

The sound of hand on flesh falls across my body like a whip.

I've been whipped before. Begged for floggers and even a single tail. But there's something in the heaviness of that hand—unwanted. Inescapable. It squeezes my heart with the same pressure as my finger, and I try to jerk away again.

Then there's a sound so familiar now that I straighten and look to the window. The thud of chopping. But the wood is too soft. It thuds instead of cracking. Squishes instead of splitting.

"We're not like that," I whisper, yanking my hand back. This time my finger pops free. Red streaks run down it, and pain rushes in as the scrapes bead up with blood. The chopping stops, and my heart slowly steadies.

"You want to save me," I murmur to the room, cradling my finger to my chest. I turn to look at Philip, sleeping like a starfish. "But I don't need to be saved."

"What did you do to your finger?" Philip demands when he wakes up.

I've cleaned the scrape, but I couldn't find any bandages, and the second knuckle has turned a deep purple, almost black.

"It's not as bad as it looks," I say, even though it's throbbing.

"It looks like you might need a doctor. What happened?"

I shake my head. If I tell him the truth, he'll insist my mind is acting up. He'll get worried that I'm losing touch with reality. Maybe I am, but I can't stand to see that look of pity in his eyes again. Not right now. "I shut it in a cupboard."

"Did the cupboard have teeth?" He gives a short bark of laughter.

I laugh with him.

"Come here." He pulls me to the bed and raises my hand by the wrist, examining the scrape more closely. "I don't like it, but I guess you're right. There's not much we can do until we get out of here. I wonder if Atanas and I could manage the tree on our own."

"It's fine," I repeat. "It doesn't even hurt."

"Okay." He gives my palm a light kiss. "I'll trust you."

My stomach flips with guilt, and I look away, pulling my knees to my chest.

"Silvena?" He leans in, angling up to see my face. "Something's definitely wrong. Tell me."

I tuck my head into my legs and take a deep breath, then I uncurl. "Can we do a scene?"

He curls a hand around my ankle. Compared to Atanas, his fingers feel cold. "Maybe. First tell me what this is about."

Shame numbs my lips. But also guilt. Because I know if I tell him, he'll take this away from me, and I'm not ready to let go of this delusion. "I can't."

"Then we can't do a scene."

"Please," I whisper. "I … need it."

My voice sounds distant. The whole room swims before me.

Philip tucks my hair behind my ear. "You know the rules. I can't give that to you if you can't share why you need it."

Tears well in my eyes and my throat grows thick. "I'm just so confused."

He pulls me to him. His arms are familiar. Not as powerful as Atanas', but familiar, and all the strength I need.

"I know, baby." He rocks me gently, and the tears spill down my cheeks. When a sob chokes out, he squeezes me tighter. "I know."

I cry until the tears run dry and my head pounds more than my finger. All the while, he just holds me, not trying to quiet me or find out why I'm crying. Eventually, I crack the cocoon of our embrace and wipe the snot from my nose with the back of my hand.

"Feel better?"

I nod, my head splitting with the motion. "But I definitely need an ibuprofen."

He smooths my hair and wipes my face. "I think we need to get out of here. This place isn't good for you. I should've been listening better."

"But the tree."

"Fuck the tree," he says. "We'll leave early, hike into town, and hitch a ride from there. A bus or train in the next city, and we'll be home by tomorrow night."

A weight lifts off my chest, as if this whole week has been a too-long session of breath play and I'm finally given the chance to suck air into my lungs. I grow giddy with the lightness in my head. "Okay. Let's do it."

CHAPTER TEN

Sleeping after a good cry is almost as good as sleeping after a scene. My dreams are non-existent. I float in an abyss, aware of every inch of my body, though my mind is unconscious. I revel in those hours, feeling the nearness of Philip beside me, his warmth a blanket of safety.

But sometime in the early morning, the bed shifts and his body leaves me. A few minutes later, I hear the clinking of his belt.

"Where are you going?" I mumble through the thickness of sleep.

"Fire's out. I have to get more wood."

I rub my eyes and look at the basket that seemed to never end. It's empty except for a few splinters of kindling. My heart thuds in my chest like the wet thump of the wood splitting I heard last night.

A spike of terror cuts through my peace. "No!"

"Silvena, it'll get cold. I'll just go down to the living room and get some. I won't be gone long."

"Please, don't." I cling to his arm like a little kid. "Stay here. It's almost dawn. We can keep each other warm for a few more hours."

"It'll be a long hike, we need our rest." He's pulling on his sweatshirt. Nothing I say will stop him. I say it anyway.

"I think Atanas … he wants to hurt you."

"Hurt me?" he frowns. "Why would he want to hurt me."

"He wants me to stay here. With him. Alone."

His eyes go wide. "He told you this?"

I nod. "He asked me to be his wife."

"And you didn't tell me?"

"I …" I stutter. "I … didn't think you'd believe me."

"No wonder you were so messed up last night. That asshole."

"I'm sorry," I say, shrinking away from his anger.

He cools immediately. "It's not your fault. He's the one overstepping boundaries. I definitely want to give him a piece of my mind, but you don't have to worry about it. He's not here."

"Right," I say to the cold room and the moon over Phil's shoulder. "Of course."

"You stay snuggled up," he says, tucking me in. "I'll be back before you know it."

I lie in silence, listening to the stairs groan as he makes his way down them. Old houses are so alive when filled with young people—all creaks and groans. They spread to make room for us. There's a shuffling below me, and then a low curse. Than a rattle and a louder curse. I recognize the front door sticking, and I can feel the entire wall rattle as Philip jerks it several times until it pops loose. Five seconds of thick silence, then a slight crunching of footsteps beneath the window. Then there's more rattling and jerking, and I realize he's trying to get into the cellar.

I let my eyes close and try to not imagine women holding their breath beside me.

There's a splintering. A pop.

A scream splits the night. Deeper than the women, and loud enough to echo off the trees. It fills the small house.

"Philip?" I whisper.

The scream turns to a gurgle.

Thwack. Thwack.

That same too-wet sound.

Then silence.

I fling the blankets off and run to the window. It sticks when I try to open it. I pull harder, bracing myself and pushing up against it. I grunt, but it won't budge. I press my forehead against the cold pane. Below me, the cellar door hangs open, but there's no sign of Philip.

"Damn it, Philip." I pull on my sweats and sweatshirt. I don't bother with socks, but head downstairs, my heart pounding, muttering, "This better not be a joke."

The front door is still open a crack. The wood has swollen so much it has trouble shutting. I don't bother forcing it, instead shoving my feet into sneakers and stumbling into the cold night.

"Philip," I whisper-hiss. "Where are you?"

Nothing.

"Philip," I call louder as I round the corner.

I slow as I approach the open door. My heart jumps into my throat, pushing up bile, but I swallow it down.

"Hello?" I ease the door open wider. Despite the full moon, no light shines into the gaping hole. I press my hand into the darkness, and it disappears fully, as if cut off.

I yank my hand back and hold it close to my stomach. "Phil, this isn't funny."

I step into the room, my foot hitting a pile of wood, sending a sound like a rippling xylophone echoing in the small space as the pile settles. I jump back, in case it falls on me, but the wood settles quickly enough, leaving me in a thick silence that doesn't smell quite like pine. Nor oak.

Another step into the room. My eyes begin to adjust to the pitch dark. The pile takes shape, a large rectangle of carefully stacked wood almost as tall as me. My foot kicks against something soft on the ground.

"Philip?" I kneel, feeling with my hands.

"No, no," I whisper, my hands patting what is definitely a leg. I clutch his loose pants, following them up to his pockets. His t-shirt hangs wet on him. The liquid is still warm. My fingers recognize his broad chest as I trace up, and then the scruff that has grown on his square jaw these last few days. I swallow and feel higher. His cheekbones. My hands tremble, fluttering off his skin like a butterfly that doesn't want to land. But I force myself to feel higher, to the cavity that was once his skull, now warm and wet and too soft.

"This isn't real," I whisper.

But he's not here to tell me it's not real. The lips of the corpse can't move. His hands can't hold me down until I see sense.

I bite my lip and look away. My eyes have started to adjust to the darkness and I can see the pile I knocked into is yellowish. Too pale to be wood. Too smooth. I edge towards it, straining my eyes in the darkness. My hand reaches out and I stroke hard, cold bone, piled high.

My ears echo with cracking. Splintering too sharp to be wood.

I stumble out of the cellar and vomit into the bushes.

CHAPTER ELEVEN

It's time to leave. Now.

I force myself off my knees and wipe the vomit from my lips. I stumble through the night, back to the house. I don't want to go through the open door, but I need the car keys. It'll get me at least to the bridge faster, putting distance between me and this cursed place.

I make it to the kitchen and root through the bags, waiting for the heavy clink of metal on metal. Didn't Philip unload here last? Wouldn't they be on the counter, hidden in our mess of groceries?

But they're not here.

I take a deep breath and try to steady myself. Upstairs? Outside in his jeans? On his …

The fire pops in the next room, and I jump. I realize the house which was freezing just moments ago is now so warm my sweater is uncomfortable.

I pull a drawer open and search for a knife. It's dull—the same one that brutalized the tomatoes—but its white plastic handle feels solid in my weak fingers.

I move into the tiny hall. Atanas stands next to the stairs, all amusement gone from his eyes, replaced by a sorrow so deep I gag just looking at it. The door I left open is closed behind him. He's fully clothed—a state I haven't seen him in for the past few days—and I hate his mountain clothes. I hate his thin height. His sharp chin and the wrinkles at the corners of his eyes turn my stomach.

"Silvena," he says.

I back up until I'm against the wall.

"You … you killed him."

"He was hurting you."

I shake my head. "You're not real."

"I'm real. You know I'm real. And you know he was hurting you."

"No!"

The large knot in the living room is smoldering again. It's grown to the size of an actual head, the features outlined in coal-red flames.

"He hurts you," it hisses.

I grip the knife tighter. "You don't understand. He doesn't hurt me."

"I watched him hit you." Atanas takes a step towards me, but I press harder into the wall.

"We saw," the knot whispers.

"That's something I ask of him."

"No one should give that to you." He takes another step. "Even if you beg for it."

The wall gapes further, hissing. "We witnessed."

"It's my choice." I grip the knife, holding it up to my shoulder. "And you took that from me. My choice. My— You took him from me."

The fire cracks again, sending a zip through my nerves, but this time I don't jump. My gaze falls on the flames in the open fireplace. The logs are thin and white, and when they split, yellow marrow oozes out.

"He didn't understand you." Atanas' voice is low and sad. "He lied to you. About me. About the things you see that he couldn't. He was strangling your gift."

"My gift?" I spit. "Anything to do with you spirits is a curse."

His eyes soften, and for a moment I see the man I haven't been able to resist for the past week, and the desire to hold him grows through my rage and fear. But I swallow it down. He killed my lover.

I look up to the wood-paneled ceiling. "And the bones in the cellar? What did those men do? Or are they the bones of the women you couldn't transform?"

He takes another step. He's arms distance away from me. Still too far for me to slash at, but close enough that he could pounce on me. I coil my muscles, ready for motion.

"I can't stand to see a woman hurt."

The screams grow louder filling the entire house.

"They're in pain," I whisper. "You're hurting them."

"They were in pain when they were alive." He reaches out and strokes my face. "I freed them."

I bring the knife down, but there's no force behind it. The blade follows the curve of Atanas' shirt, falling flat against his chest. "You trapped them here. Just so you wouldn't be alone. Your wives."

I spit the word wives into his face.

He wipes the wet from his cheek and stares at me with infinite patience. "They weren't like you. Not as strong. With you, it'll be different."

I close my eyes as he folds me against his chest. I hear Philip telling me, so many times through the years. "You're stronger than you think. You're stronger than any hand that has touched you. Stronger than me. The things you've lived through ... you're one of the strongest people I know."

I hold my breath, wait to feel Atanas against me, then

duck beneath his arm, bolting for the door. I reach it before he can grab me, and I yank on the handle.

It doesn't budge.

I pull harder. He should be on me by now, but when I chance a glance over my shoulder, he's still standing at the end of the hall, watching me struggle.

"Let me out," I say.

"No," he answers. "I won't let you go."

I stop struggling and let my forehead fall against the door. "You could have had us both. You didn't have to kill him."

"He would have convinced you you're insane and taken you away from here." He wraps his hands around me, and he's warm as the fire. I begin sweating, turning my pajamas damp. "I couldn't allow that."

The screaming stops. There's silence except for the crackling of the fire.

"Be with me."

"You said I needed to agree, that you wouldn't force me."

"I can't you force you." His voice is barely a whisper. "But I can't let you go."

There's nothing left but spirits and fires and screaming women. It's life as a knot of wood, or burning as a pile of bones. Or maybe he's right. Philip, too. Maybe I'm stronger than I think. I release the doorknob and let Atanas lead me into the living room.

"What happens now?" I ask. But I know. I've seen it a dozen times in the past week. A woman being flayed. Her skin splitting open and dropping to the ground like a discarded dress.

"I'll turn you into Kikimora. My final bride," Atanas

says. "And neither of us will be alone."

He's standing before me, holding my hands loosely. The wrinkles around his eyes crinkle with sincerity, and despite my fear, forgetting my hate, I feel pity and pain swell in me.

"Can you stoke the fire?" I ask with a quiver in my voice. "I'm cold."

"You won't be cold for long," he says. But he turns his back to me and lays more logs on the fire, pulling the bones out of thin air. He no longer bothers turning them into wood. All pretenses have fallen.

The knife rests behind me on the table, and I wonder if it would do anything if I sunk it into his back. Can you kill an apparition?

I glance to the face on the wall. Her mouth is closed, lips pressed into a thin line. An ember rolls down from what might be her eye, burning a black streak into the wood.

He turns to me. "Are you ready?"

"Will it hurt?" It's a stupid question. I felt it in the forest, bark being peeled like skin.

His eyes swell with sympathy. "I'll make it quick."

He moves in, hesitant at first, then sighs and covers my mouth with his. His tongue tastes of ash. Of the sky turned orange and swathes of forest burned to the ground. My lungs fill with a deep, spicy smoke, and I almost pull away to cough, but he pins me against his chest. He kisses me deeper, opening my throat. The taste chokes me, but beneath the forest fire, there's the hint of new growth. The nuttiness of seeds. Dew on charcoal. Dirt with worms and microbes that won't be killed.

He takes off my shirt and I step out of my pants. He's naked, and I'm not sure when or how that happened, but it doesn't matter. I run my hands through the fur of his chest.

It's summer moss. A winter coat of pine needles that mute the forest. This time I'm the one to reach up and bring our mouths together.

As he grows against my belly, our kiss deepens. His fingers clench my shoulder blades, then pull down.

Sharp nails, too long to be human and as hard as steel, slice into my skin. It stings worse than a single tail. I hiss into his mouth, but he does not release me, continuing to draw eight slices from my shoulders down to my buttocks.

I whimper into his mouth.

"It'll be over soon," he promises. It was always over soon. The women stepped out of their bodies. Too weak. Pressed into wood for safekeeping. Like a flower plucked from a meadow. Nothing more than a keepsake to remember a summer he couldn't hold.

He runs his nails down my back again, and blood smears hot over my skin. The sharp pain grows numb. He pulls his hand around to the front, slicing my side and belly. I make the mistake of looking down. There's nothing human about the gnarled claw caressing me. He moves it between my legs, spreading them, and I comply. Despite everything he's done, there's still a part of me that wants him.

I pull his gnarled cock into me before guilt can incapacitate me.

The pain dulls with every thrust. I'm taken further away. A single tree being chopped down. It's separated from the roots that run the vast width of the forest. It groans.

Atanas groans.

I groan and prop my foot against a chair.

He thrusts again, and I tip the chair back. The top just barely reaches the fireplace, inches away from the flame.

Atanas thrusts again, and there's a final split in the wood.

The endless falling of a tree.

Loneliness like I've never felt before washes through me. I buck beneath it, spasming at the pain.

I push the chair further until it catches flame.

Then I kiss away Atanas' pain as best I can.

"You're not alone," my tongue promises as he presses deep into me. I clench around him, slowing his motion.

He continues shredding me, but I no longer feel my body. My skin is a mass of lacerations and blood puddles on the floor.

But my eyes remain open, staring over his shoulder as his endless fire eats through the chair, catching the wooden floor boards. It surrounds us, licking up the table as Atanas gives a final tear to my chest.

I open to the room and the wound is cold and hot and sweet and painful. I can feel my soul being drawn from my body, into Atanas' arms. Except his arms have disappeared.

He has become the nothingness. The abyss.

The fire burns around us and he swirls on its heat.

"What have you done?" he asks.

But he knows. The beams above us crash to the floor, the house crumbling as the fire rises. The wood crackles and hisses and ancient steam flows from it, turning into a miniature tornado. A dust devil. My devil.

"As long as this wood stands," I repeat to him.

Another beam crashes. Flames shoot into the early morning sky.

"Come with me," he says, swirling just above the mess of the house.

I feel the stones the house was built upon. The bones in the cellar. The women that have become nothing more than ash. I reach up to the cold night sky, but my body continues to burn below, and I can't bring myself to leave it.

"No," I say.

"No?" He hesitates.

"You belong to the trees, but I belong to these bones."

He whirls down to me like a swarm of gnats, solidifying just enough to embrace my crisped corpse as I return to it. "Thank you, Kiki."

As I burn to ash, my spirit melting into the foundation of stone, I let him call me Kiki, because sometimes the things we imagine are more important than those that are real.

ABOUT THE AUTHOR

KOJI A. DAE is a queer, synesthetic American living long-term in Bulgaria with her husband, two kids, and a cat. She is enthralled by Eastern European mythology and, after ten years of soaking up the magic of the Balkan Mountains, she feels prepared to write about it. By day she works with a non-profit furthering Bulgarian education, and by night she reads, writes, and crochets. Her short fiction can be found in *Clarkesworld Magazine*, *Apex Magazine* and others, and she has a poetry collection called *Scars that Never Bled: An Exploration of Frankenstein Through Poetry*.

Find Koji on Twitter / X @kojiadae or at kojiadae.ink.

WINTER
HARVEST
IOANNA PAPADOPOULOU

"T.L. BODINE'S NOVEL GRIPPED ME THROUGHOUT."
—ALLY WILKES
NEVEREST
T.L. BODINE

The
BELLADONNA
INVITATION
ROSE BIGGIN